W9-AQO-050

Up in Seth's Room

Up in Seth's Room

A Love Story by
NORMA FOX MAZER

DELACORTE PRESS/NEW YORK

Published by
Delacorte Press
1 Dag Hammarskjold Plaza
New York, N.Y. 10017

Manufactured in the United States of America

First printing

Designed by MaryJane DiMassi

LIBRARY OF CONGRESS CATALOGING IN PUBLICATION DATA

Mazer, Norma Fox, 1931–
Up in Seth's room.

SUMMARY: A 15-year-old's first love is
bittersweet as she defies her parents and tries to
assert her sexual values.
I.   Title.
PZ7.M47398Up   [Fic]   79-2102
ISBN 0-440-08920-4

First he taught her. Then she taught him. It was like a race where they passed the baton from one to the other. Then they took it together and ran.

1

Finn Rousseau looked up at her sister's third-floor window, suddenly almost reluctant to see Maggie. She brushed snow off her jeans. People never shoveled their walks in this neighborhood, and the three blocks from the bus had been knee-deep in last night's fall. She stamped the snow from her boots. Delaying tactics. In the back of her mind she was aware she'd built up her expectations for this visit to the point where she was sure to be disappointed.

What if Jim was there? He probably would be. He lived there, didn't he? And he was on vacation from school, too. Even if he wasn't there, Maggie would be talking about him.

Finn threw her striped scarf over her shoulder. It was ridiculous standing on the street this way. She *had* to go up, if for nothing more than to borrow Maggie's velvet skirt for the New Year's Eve party that night. She went up the front steps and into the vestibule. It was an old building with remnants of former dignity. There was a row of brass mailboxes on one wall. She found Maggie's name—ROUSSEAU: next to it, connected with a dash, WARENECKE. ROUSSEAU-WARENECKE, as if it were one name.

All the way over on the bus she'd thought of nothing but how she and Maggie were going to be together for a few hours, just the two of them, talking about anything that came to mind: their parents, Finn's school, Maggie's job, clothes, sex, or money. The subject wouldn't matter. What would count would be that she and Maggie fall back into their old easy ways together. That Finn be able to tell Maggie, *Since you left home, it's not the same.* And that Maggie say, *I know, Finnsey, I know. . . .*

She went up the steps two at a time. Right after her fifteenth birthday in May she'd grown four inches. She had very long legs, was five feet nine, and taller than her mother. Coltish, her mother called her, but sometimes Finn felt horse-ish would be more appropriate. She just wasn't delicate like a colt. Besides, when she smiled, she felt that she showed a lot of teeth. And on top of that there was her mane of straw-colored hair which she (naturally) wore in a horsetail.

"I hope you're not in, Jim," she muttered, starting up the second flight. "No offense, Jim." Jim was okay. Finn wasn't crazy about him, but since Maggie was, he was all right with Finn. It was just that she'd hardly seen her sister in the past four months. And come to think of it, when she had seen her, it had never been alone.

Not such a terrific record considering how close they used to be. Despite Maggie's being five years older, they'd been good friends for as long as Finn could remember—sharing a bedroom, their closet, cosmetics, and clothes, their good moods and bad.

Even last year, when Maggie was going with Jim and spending most of her free time with him, she and Finn still found time to talk. And, Finn had always thought, told each other just about everything. At least she told Maggie everything. But the fact was, as Finn had realized, Maggie had had her own private life for a long time before she moved out of their house.

Maggie's door was painted bright green. Finn tattooed a knock on the door. A moment later it was opened, and there was Maggie, wearing a V-neck green sweater over jeans, and a printed green kerchief over her springy red curls. "Maggie!" It was so good to see her sister.

She hugged Maggie. "You look gorgeous! Green must be your favorite—" She stopped short. Over Maggie's shoulder she saw two strangers in the apartment. A guy sitting on the couch, and a short plump girl looking through Maggie's records.

"Finn," her sister said, drawing her into the living room, "this is Toby, and this is Seth. Hey, you guys, this is my sister, Finn. Toby and Seth just drove up from Auburn, Finn. Seth is Jim's brother."

Finn almost fell over. She knew Jim had a brother. She'd even heard Jim's brother was the family black sheep—a high school dropout. Everything Jim Ware-necke, Jr.—the successful young med student—wasn't. All the same, she'd imagined Jim's younger brother would somehow be the same sort of buttoned-up, roly-poly type as Jim.

But Seth was lean and dark, and the way he was sit-ting on the couch, legs crossed, hands resting gracefully on his thighs, he looked more like a prince out of a fairy tale than any dropout Finn knew. Except, of course, for the faded jeans and scuffed work boots.

"Hello, Finn," he said. He had a great voice! Deep and warm.

"Hello," she said. God! He was good-looking enough for half a dozen guys. She dropped into the beanbag chair near the window.

"Did you walk here?" Toby said to her. "Do you live near Maggie?" She fingered the gold chain around her neck.

"I took a bus," Finn said. "We live across town, then I walked—"

But Toby had turned to Seth and was asking him if he remembered the time they had walked twenty miles on a March Against Hunger. "Remember, it rained all day? And we were soaked . . . like, *wet*," Toby said, laughing, and jangling an armful of bracelets.

Maggie went into the kitchen. "I'll get us something to drink," she said.

"You got blisters on your feet that day," Seth said to Toby.

"Did I ever! It hurts just to remember."

Finn sank deeper into the beanbag chair. She tried

to think of something to say. *Say nothing,* she advised herself. *No one's interested.* She dug her battered copy of *Wuthering Heights* out of her pocket. *At fifteen,* she read (not for the first time, since this was absolutely her favorite book), *she was the queen of the countryside; she had no peer; and she did turn out a haughty, headstrong creature!* Finn loved that passage, loved Catherine. Nobody monkeyed around with Catherine!

"Refreshments, people." Maggie carried in a tray with Cokes and a box of Cheese Puffs.

"Mmm!" Toby dipped into the Cheese Puffs. "Seth—?" He took a handful, tipped up his head, and threw the Puffs into his mouth one by one.

"Bravo, bravo." Toby applauded.

Seth smiled. Bet anything he knows how good-looking he is, Finn thought. All that dark hair and those high cheekbones and full, red lips. She decided she didn't like him. Tooo, tooo, *too* good-looking.

"Cheese Puffs, Finn?" Toby said.

Finn shook her head. "No thanks."

"No wonder you're skinny."

"I just don't like Cheese Puffs," Finn said.

"I'll get something else for you next time," Maggie said. She opened a Coke. "Seth's going to stay with Jim and me for a while, Finn. He's going to get a job in Syracuse."

"If it's okay with Jim," Seth said.

"It'll be okay with Jim," Maggie said confidently. "You'll sleep right on the couch. No problem." She turned to Finn. "Let me go look for that skirt before

I do anything else." She went into the bedroom, and Toby went to get a glass for her Coke. Seth and Finn were alone.

"How was the drive from Auburn?" she said, making conversation.

"Fine," he said.

"How long did it take you?"

"About half an hour."

"Oh, yes." She nodded politely. She kept staring at him. She couldn't help it.

Then for a minute neither of them said anything. She looked down at her book.

"Good book?" he said.

"Yeah. Really."

"You must be on vacation now."

"Right. It's almost over, though. Three more days."

"I always liked winter vacation especially," he said. "Loafing around the house and eating crazy things."

"I know what you mean," she said, laughing.

Toby had come back. "Soooo!" She set her Coke glass down on the arm of the couch and sat down next to Seth. "You're Maggie's little sister?" She put her arm through Seth's.

"Right," Finn said crisply. Bitch, she thought. Don't worry, I'm not trying to take away your gorgeous boyfriend. She got up and started plucking dead leaves off Maggie's plants. The window was full of hanging plants, and more plants were sitting in pots and crocks on the floor.

"You two don't look at all alike," Toby said.

"No, we don't."

"Maggie's beautiful."

"Yes, she is. I agree."

"You're not jealous?" Toby sipped her Coke. "I thought sisters were jealous of each other."

"Maggie and I are friends." Finn snipped a spindly stalk on a polka-dot plant.

"How nice." Toby smiled at Finn like a kindly kindergarten teacher. In fact, Finn learned in a moment, Toby *was* a future kindergarten teacher, doing her training in one of the Auburn elementary schools. "I love it," she said, getting back to Toby—the subject that obviously really interested her. The kids were great and *loved* her. Also, she *loved* winter because she loved skiing, and she was really a good skier.

A remote look crossed Seth's face. Finn wondered if he'd heard all this before. How close were he and Toby, anyway? Not that Finn cared, but it was an interesting speculation. Toby was hanging on him, but he seemed fairly cool.

Maggie came back, brushing off the velvet skirt. "I found it, Finn." She held it up for Finn's approval, then dropped it on the beanbag chair. "Come on, sit down," she said, sitting down on the floor herself. "Stop bothering my plants." Then, in the special, ironic tone of voice she'd used for their parents ever since the big, awful blowup in September, when she'd moved out, Maggie said, "And how is my mother? And my father?"

"They're fine," Finn said, leaning against the wall.

"Do they ask about me?"

"Maggie. You know how they feel." Finn glanced at Toby. She didn't want to talk about their family problems in front of strangers. It seemed disloyal. "You could come over, Maggie," she said guardedly. "Just stop in, it would make Mom feel good."

"Why doesn't she come over here?" Maggie said.

"You know—" Finn said.

"She's afraid she'll be contaminated," Maggie said. "The sin I'm living in might be catching."

"Come on, Maggie," Finn said. "You know it isn't like that. She and Dad just don't think it's right, the way you and Jim—" She broke off, having said more than she meant to. At home (to her parents) she defended Maggie's right to live any way she wanted to. Here, she defended her parents to Maggie. Sometimes she felt like a piece of taffy being pulled from both sides. "Mom misses you," she said.

"Oh, ho-ho."

"No, she does, Maggie."

Maggie oh-ho-hoed again. She turned to Seth and Toby. "Listen to this, you two. Right after Jim and I moved in together, I called home. My darling parents hung up on me!"

"That was Dad," Finn said. "Not Mom. Fair's fair, Mag. You know how Dad is. He gets mad, but he gets over it."

"You don't have to alibi for them," Maggie said. "When it comes to Jim and me, Mom and Dad are Tweedledum and Tweedledee."

"No, I've heard Mom crying at night," Finn said.

Maggie sat up very straight. "Did she send you here with that message? Wow, it's like pressing the right button. On comes the recording about how much I'm making my mother suffer."

Jesus! Talk about bitchiness. Flushing, Finn shoved

her book into her hip pocket. What was she doing hanging around here? Toby, bored probably, picked up a magazine, but Seth was taking in all the juicy details.

"Listen, Maggie, I'm nobody's errand girl." Finn grabbed her jacket and the velvet skirt, threw her scarf around her neck and started for the door. "Thanks for the skirt. I'm going home."

"Hey, Finnsey—"

"No! Don't 'Finnsey' me. I get it from Mom and Dad, Maggie, and I get it from you, and I'm sick of being in the middle." Her face was hot, she spoke with passion, too much passion, she thought. She was making a fool of herself, but she couldn't stop. Not even when she saw Jim's brother looking right at her.

"It's okay with me if you're living with Jim, I think it's great, but it's not so great living with our parents the way they feel. You just went out of the house, Maggie, took your stuff and left, and that was it. You didn't think about what you were leaving behind."

There was a little silence. Then Maggie stood up. "I didn't mean to insult you." She held out her hands. "Come on, sit down."

"I'll miss my bus," Finn said. Hell. Why hadn't she exited on her big exit line? *I'm going home.*

"There's always another bus," her sister said.

"Sounds profound," Seth said. He smiled at Finn. "A whole philosophy of life." She could see he was being nice, trying to smooth over things.

Maggie took Finn's hands. "You know me, always shooting off my mouth."

"You sure do," Finn said.

"I humbly apologize." Maggie bowed. "I deeply,

humbly, *sincerely* apologize." She put a record on the stereo. Joni Mitchell, Finn's favorite singer. "The wind is in from Africa, /Last night I couldn't sleep ..." Joni sang in her heartbreaking voice.

Finn sat down again, glancing at Seth. Had she acted like a jerk? She was still upset.

Toby looked at her gold wristwatch. "Time for me to go." She zipped up her leather boots. "It was great seeing you again, Maggie."

"Come on down, any time," Maggie said.

Seth stood and put an arm around Toby's neck. "Thanks for the ride. I appreciate it."

"It was nothing, sweetie." She took his chin in her hands and kissed him on the mouth. She said good-bye to Maggie, waved vaguely in Finn's direction, and left.

It was getting dark outside. In a while Finn got ready to leave. "Nice meeting you," she said to Seth.

"Guess we'll be seeing each other sometimes," he said. "Since I'll be living here for a while."

Finn wanted to say, I hope so . . . or, That would be great. She actually liked him better than she'd first thought. But she didn't say anything, just smiled. He smiled back, then held out his hand and, a bit awkwardly, they shook.

Maggie followed Finn out into the dark hall, saying, "Don't be such a stranger. Come over more. We're sisters, aren't we?"

Finn went down a few steps, then looked up. Maggie looked so young leaning over the banister, younger than twenty, with her headful of red curls and wide-open blue eyes. "You're not still mad at me, are you?" she said to Finn.

Finn shook her head. "No, I guess I sounded off." After a moment she said, "How old is Seth?"

"Nineteen."

Finn whistled. "He's cute."

"I know, he really is. I like him, but he's nothing like Jim. They don't look alike, they don't sound alike, they don't think alike." Maggie laughed.

"Maggie," Finn said, "are you happy?"

Maggie nodded solemnly. "I am, Finn. I really am."

"I'm glad," Finn said. "I want you to be happy. But maybe it would be better . . . if you were married?"

Maggie made a face. "Cut it out. We'll get married some day. Maybe when Jim is through school and his residency requirements. We've got plenty of time."

Finn nodded. Now, on the stairs, they were having the sort of talk she'd imagined them having in Maggie's apartment. Just the two of them, close, and saying what they really felt. "I just wish you could come home."

"Not without Jim," Maggie said.

"I know. I meant you and Jim."

"And we could bring along Seth," Maggie said mischievously.

Finn laughed. "I've got to go," she said, "or I really will miss my bus." But she kept lingering, looking up at Maggie. "Thanks for the skirt. I'll return it in perfect condition." She ran down the steps.

Outside the stars were just appearing in the sky. The snow layered on the trees, the ice-cold stars, and the blue dusk settling over the old building made Finn ache inside. It was so good to be alive. She glanced up at Maggie's window again. Was Seth looking out? Impulsively, just in case he was, she waved.

2

"Who do you like, Finn?" Karen Barnowski, the little girl who lived next door, sat on Finn's bed, watching her put on eye shadow. Karen had come over a few minutes before to say that her sister, Vida, said Finn should be ready to leave for Cindy's New Year's Eve party in twenty minutes. Cindy Waller's crowd was older and cooler than most of the kids Finn knew well. It was because she was Vida's friend that Finn had been invited. Vida was a year older than Finn. Now that the party was nearly upon her, she was nervous.

"What'd you say, Karen?" Wearing her bra and Maggie's red velvet skirt, Finn leaned toward the mirror, dabbing on blue eye shadow with a shaky hand.

"I said," Karen repeated patiently, "Who do you like? Who is your lover in the world?"

Finn blinked soggily. Her brush had slipped and half

the shadow had landed on her lashes. "You have a neat way of putting things, Karen."

"Is it a secret?" Karen chewed the end of a braid. "If you tell me, I'll tell you my boyfriend."

"I didn't know you had a boyfriend, Karen."

"I do. His name is Eddy Lister. I call him Eddy Blister."

"Eddy Blister! You never told me that before." Finn pulled down her other eyelid and began working on it.

"You have a boyfriend, too," Karen sang out.

"No, I don't," Finn sang back.

"Vida says! Vida says! Jerry Demas, that's who. At the party tonight."

"No, Vida never said any such thing, Karen. No boyfriend, and *definitely* not Jerry Demas." Jerry Demas was a year ahead of Finn, the kind of guy whose eyes danced all over a girl, especially her breasts.

"Vida said so," Karen insisted. "You and Jerry."

Finn slipped her arms into a long-sleeved, cream-colored blouse. What was going on? Was Vida trying to pair her up with Jerry? They'd hardly ever even spoken.

"Looks good, honey," her mother said, peering into the room. "Hi, Karen." Mrs. Rousseau was in her bathrobe but still wearing her white nurses' shoes. She'd come home about half an hour ago, after working overtime at General Hospital in the Indian Hills. "Glad someone in this family is going to celebrate the new year the right way."

"Poor Mom," Finn said, doing up the last few buttons on the blouse. "Maybe Dad will get home tonight." Her father was a trucker for Roadway.

"That would be too much to expect," her mother said. "No, I don't think so. Maybe tomorrow, if we're lucky." She ran her hand through her hair, the same curly red hair as Maggie's. "I'm beat. I'm going to take a long hot soak. Have a nice time, honey, and don't come home too late."

"I won't," Finn said.

"You're sure that Paul is going to walk you and Vida home?"

"Positive, Mom. I won't come home alone."

The doorbell rang. Three short rings. Vida's signal. Finn started to put on her coat, then paused. "How do I look, Karen? Do I look all right?"

Karen walked all around her. "You look nice as mice."

Finn and Karen went downstairs. Vida, buttoned up to the chin in a heavy, dark blue coat, was waiting outside. "I was just coming up to get you," she said to Finn. And to Karen, "Go on home, Mom wants you." She caught Finn's arm, and they walked together.

"That looks like a policeman's coat," Finn said.

"It is," Vida said. "You know my uncle, Danny Barnowski? It's his old cop coat. Mom remodeled it."

"You could wear anything and look good," Finn said. It was Vida's coloring—her skin and hair were creamy, like butterscotch mixed with milk.

They walked toward Salina Street, the salt street, as Finn liked to think of it. She loved the names of the streets in her neighborhood: Turtle Street, Bear Street, Wolf Street, Butternut Street, Pond Street. The houses were plain and comfortable, with porches and lots of windows. Colored Christmas lights were strung up across the fronts and draped around trees in the yards.

In a few days the curbs would be littered with discarded Christmas trees.

"What time is Paul coming to the party?" Finn said.

"About ten."

It was a deeply cold night. The stars sparkled icily, and the snow crunched underfoot. Both girls were carrying their shoes in bags.

"I went to see Maggie yesterday," Finn said, "and I met Jim's brother, Seth." She liked saying his name. "You should see Seth, Vida. He's gorgeous."

"Where does he go to school?"

"He doesn't."

"How old is he? Does he go to college?"

"No, he works, I mean he's looking for work. That's why he's here. I guess he lives in Auburn, usually. But—"

"Oh, I knew I had something to tell you," Vida said, interrupting. "A certain person is going to be at the party looking for you. Initials J. D."

"Let me see, who could that be?" Finn said innocently.

"You'll never guess."

"Give me a try. Jerry Demas?"

"Finn! How'd you know?"

"Karen told me."

"The little fink! I should never tell her anything."

Finn laughed. "You leave Karen alone. She's my favorite little spy."

"Well, since you know . . . what do you think of Jerry?"

"I don't even know him, Vida. How come he's going to be looking for me, anyway? I don't believe that."

"He likes you," Vida said. "He and Paul and I were all in Paul's father's store in the Mall the other day, and I just casually slipped your name into the conversation. I said something about how much fun you were. And guess what? Jerry said he's looked you over, he's noticed you in school, and he likes what he sees. I think he's adorable, Finn! I think he'd be great to go with."

"Superman has nothing on you, Vida. I haven't even said hello to him, and you've got us going together. You move with the speed of light." Finn didn't take all this too seriously. Guys were always saying things. "Anyway, I thought he and Terri Lyon went together."

"They broke up. I'll tell you something. If I didn't have Paul, I'd go all out for Jerry. Don't you love those sleepy brown eyes of his?"

"Don't let Paul hear you saying that."

"Oh, don't worry, Paul and I are like the Rock of Gibraltar."

"Vida, does your mother ever suspect that you and Paul are having sex?"

"We're careful! I don't believe in being careless. You have to think of things in advance. We don't take chances. We plan everything. There are so many little details you have to take care of."

Discussing her arrangements to make love with Paul, Vida's voice had the same tone as it did when she told Finn how she made brownies—practical and sincere. "It sounds more like work than fun," Finn said.

"Fun?" Vida repeated. "Well, if you want to have fun, you've got to do things right. What do you think?"

"I don't know," Finn said. "All I've got to go on is hearsay."

"Don't worry, Finn, your day will come."

"That day is a long way off."

"You never know," Vida said. "You could meet the right person tomorrow—or tonight."

The reference to Jerry didn't escape Finn. "I don't think so, Vida." She had a gut feeling that she and Jerry weren't the sort of people who would really get along. Still, it *was* flattering that he was looking at her. Then she thought of Jim's brother, Seth, again, and said, "Well, maybe I will meet someone great, but that doesn't mean we'll get into making love."

"Why not?" Vida said. "I bet you would." It was an old argument between them.

"Too soon. Too young. Too important," Finn said succinctly.

"I've heard that before," Vida said. "You'll change your mind. Let me tell you something, Finn. Sex is natural. It's beautiful. And sometimes it's—" She waved her shoes in the air. "It's sacred. Yes, sacred." Her voice dropped. "Sometimes, *after*, Paul and I are incredibly close. We don't need words or anything, we're really in touch with our souls."

"It's beautiful that you're so close," Finn said, a little wistfully.

"Well, we wouldn't be, without sex," Vida said. "Sometimes I think you take your attitude just out of stubbornness."

"Truce," Finn said. "You know, we're never going to agree." The funny thing she had noticed about sex was that if you said you didn't want it yet, nobody believed you.

Sure, she was curious, but she was ready to wait. Her mother hadn't ever had sex till she got married—that was carrying things too far, Finn thought. But it hadn't hurt her mother, or her marriage. Her parents had one of the best marriages Finn knew. They really loved each other. Of course they were old fashioned about a lot of things; that was why they couldn't accept Maggie's living with Jim.

"Someday," Vida said, "you're going to stand right here, Finnis Rousseau, and say, 'Vida, you were right, and I was wrong!'"

Smiling, Finn looked up at the sky. ". . . let's not talk of fare-thee-wells now/the night is a starry dome . . ." she sang under her breath. So perfect. She loved the way Joni Mitchell wrote her songs. The night sure was a starry dome!

At Cindy's house a big plastic, red-nosed Santa Claus was winking on and off in the front window. Vida and Finn pulled off their boots in the hall and put on their shoes.

"Vida! Finn! You came, that's good," Cindy said, meeting them at the door. She was a skinny, hyper blonde. "Coats in the bedroom, first door to your right. Make yourselves at home. Eat! Drink! Dance! See you all!"

In the bedroom Finn and Vida threw their coats down on the pile on the bed. Vida checked herself in the mirror. "You look great," Finn said. Vida was wearing a long, orangey-yellow dress with a brown velvet ribbon around her hair.

"You look super, too," Vida said, fingering the silver heart-locket Paul had given her for Christmas.

Finn bent down to glance at herself. A fast look: one-two-three-I-see-me. It took her by surprise. She saw a tall, flushed girl, her hair loose—someone who wasn't Maggie-beautiful, but was really attractive.

In the living room kids were dancing. There were noisemakers piled on the TV, and a table with food and punch in a big glass bowl. Right away a boy asked Vida to dance. Finn got a cup of punch and sipped it. It had a sharp aftertaste. Probably spiked.

Vida waved to her from across the room. Finn gave her a having-a-wonderful-time-by-myself look. She drank a second glass of punch. Bits of conversation floated around her.

"My horoscope never says anything good. Three times, every time I went out with Keith, it said, 'Control yourself.' Just what I can't do."

" . . . and he said, 'If that's the way you're going to be, forget it!' "

"Listen, I was so scared my knees were literally knocking together, and he . . ."

Just when her cheeks were beginning to stiffen into rigor mortis from smiling at no one, Doc Frank came over. He was the best actor in school. "Finn Rousseau," he said in his deep, theatrical voice. "You're looking charming." He was puffing on a pipe.

"I saw you in *Guys and Dolls*," she said. "You were great."

"You ever think of trying out for a play?" he said.

Finn laughed. "I don't have any acting talent. The best I could do would be an animal imitation. I do a terrific horse." The combination of punch and a little attention at last animated her. "Want to hear?" Without waiting for a reply she tossed her head, distended her nostrils, and whinnied.

Doc applauded. "Best horse I've heard in a long time."

"Nay, sir, you flatter me," Finn said.

"*Nay,* sir!" Doc chuckled so appreciatively, Finn tried to think of something else funny to say. But before she could, Vida pulled her aside.

"Finn, I have to talk to you."

"Vida!" She looked back at Doc. "I'm talking to Doc," she said.

"Doc belongs to Vicki," Vida said. "I just have a minute. Paul's here. He and Jerry came together. Jerry is going to ask you to dance." She nudged Finn. "Here he comes now. Smile, Finn, smile!"

3

"I've seen you around school," Jerry said. His dark brown eyes danced over Finn. He was wearing navy blue trousers, a blue tie, a white shirt, a gold tieband. Very collegiate, very turned out. "Dance?" he said, as if he were really suggesting something a lot more interesting and dangerous.

Off they went. Finn was nearly a head taller than Jerry. "I've watched you play basketball," she said. You're good."

Jerry nodded, acknowledging the compliment. He held her very close. "You play girls' basketball, don't you?" he said. Then, graciously, "Some of you girls are pretty good."

Wearing a gold tentlike dress, Brenda Beech danced past by herself, her heavy white arms weaving patterns in the air. "Look at Brenda," Jerry said. "What a character. She ought to lose about fifty pounds."

"Maybe she doesn't want to," Finn said.

"Are you kidding? Who'd want to be in that shape?"

"She's got an awfully pretty face."

"It wasn't her face I was looking at," Jerry said.

Finn decided to change the subject. "I didn't know you were a friend of Paul Valdone's."

"He's my third or fourth cousin." Jerry pulled her even closer. "Ever hear of kissing cousins?" He had a way of lowering his lids and glancing at her, looking her over, that was disturbing. Finn's cheeks were hot.

The record ended. They drank some more punch, then danced again. Then more punch. Jerry was staying close. The punch was tasting better all the time.

"I like tall girls," Jerry said. Then The Look, as if what he was saying was only a cover-up for what he was really thinking.

Across the room Nancy Govenda was staring at Finn and Jerry. Nancy and Finn had a long-standing, unstated rivalry. Nancy was just Jerry's size. Finn smiled over this thought as if it were profound. Jerry had both hands around her waist. They were nearly standing still, swaying to the music.

"Everybody," Brenda Beech called, clapping her hands. "Let's go outside and make a snowman." There were cheers and boos. "You guys making out in the corners need the fresh air," Brenda called. "Follow me!" She whipped a long striped scarf around her neck and sailed to the door.

Finn blinked as if she'd been half asleep. Everyone

was leaving. "I want to make a snowman," she said, smiling.

"No, let's stay in," Jerry said.

Finn shook her head. She ran out. She knew Jerry would follow her. She didn't know how she knew, but she was positive. It was cold outside, and snow was falling.

"Hush, everybody, hush! The neighbors," Cindy said, but nobody paid attention.

They rolled two huge snowballs and raised them into place. Jerry was there. He had followed her out. Brenda put her scarf around the snowman's neck. Finn stuck her tasseled wool hat on his head. Just then the church bells rang. It was midnight.

Everyone started screaming. "Happy new year! Happy new year!" Cindy and Duane Rodman grabbed each other and kissed passionately. Jerry grabbed Finn. His hand was around her neck, his legs were pressed against hers. She kissed him back hard. She was excited, but at the same time aware of a little sense of disappointment. She wanted to be swept away, but she kept hearing the other kids. Was she kissing back passionately enough?

"Let's go inside," Jerry said. Ducking around the side of the house, they went back in through the kitchen. They stamped the snow from their feet, threw their jackets on a chair. Finn's cheeks were stinging from the cold.

"Did you like that kiss?" Jerry said, taking her hand. "How about you? Did you like it?"

"Here's how I'll answer that. Do you want to go with me?" He put his arms around her.

"Go where?" she said stupidly, as if he'd invited her on a midnight stroll through the wintery streets of the city.

Jerry laughed. "Vida said you had a good sense of humor."

Finn smiled modestly.

"I think we could have fun together," he said. "Yes?" He squeezed her shoulder.

"Mmm, yes, we could have . . . ahhh . . ." She didn't want to say "fun" because the way Jerry was looking at her—sort of The Look of Looks—she was pretty sure this was a case of a three-letter word substituting for a four-letter word. She hiccuped. This struck her as wildly funny, and she giggled, realizing she was high from the punch.

"Think about it," Jerry said. "I know girls need time to make up their minds." His fingers pattered up and down her arm. "I really think we can hit it off. I like tall girls. I like girls with a sense of humor and their own minds."

She gazed at Jerry with blurry admiration. Wonderful! That he knew so clearly, so definitively, what he liked. She imagined a very tall girl carefully holding her mind, like a basketball, in front of her. "It's my own mind, of course," the girl was saying. "I never bother with strangers' minds. So tacky."

Jerry nuzzled along the line of her chin, then licked it. God, Finn thought happily, there are interesting things happening tonight.

"Let's go into the bedroom," he said.

"The bedroom," she pointed out cleverly, "has a *bed* in it."

"That's the idea." He put his arm around her and led her into a dark room off the kitchen.

"Put on the lights," Finn cried. "It's dark in here."

Jerry laughed. Finn laughed. He gave her a tug and landed them both on the bed. He put his arms around her, and they kissed again. Finn was enthusiastic. Then Jerry stuck his tongue in her mouth. It was certainly peculiar having someone else's tongue in her mouth. The thought passed through her mind that since it was her mouth and she hadn't invited in *his* tongue, it would serve him right if she chewed on it a little. But what if Jerry took that as a sign of returned passion, instead of territorial affirmative?

In another room a door banged. "Any more punch?" someone said.

"Listen." Finn drew away. "Everyone's coming in now. We better go."

"Jesus," Jerry muttered. "Just when things were starting to get interesting."

"I know, I know," Finn agreed.

He put his hand affectionately on the back of her neck. "Well, that's the breaks, kid. You'll just have to wait for another time."

The party broke up a little after one. Finn retrieved her hat from the snowman and stuck her shoes in her pocket. Jerry walked her home. Near her house he stopped by a tree, and they kissed again. He put his hands under her jacket. Finn shivered. It was so nice, having her breasts touched.

They started walking again and turned the corner

onto her street. In their driveway she saw her father's rig. "My father's home," she said. "I haven't seen him in almost two weeks."

"Where's he been?" Jerry said.

"He's a contract driver for Roadway. You know their slogan? 'Always on the road, always in the way.'" Jerry didn't laugh. "He's been down in Florida," Finn went on hastily.

"Why'd he come back?" Jerry said, kicking at a snowbank.

"He loves Syracuse. Why else?"

Jerry put his arm around her. "Next time," he said, lowering his voice and giving her The Look, "we take up where we left off."

Finn laughed. "We'll see about that," she teased. She ran into the house.

Her parents were in the kitchen, waiting up for her. They were both in bathrobes, sitting at the table with coffee cups. "Thought you weren't going to be home till tomorrow," Finn said to her father.

"I got lucky," her mother said.

Finn hugged her father. His hair was damp from the shower. He smelled good—shaving lotion and tobacco. "You smell good," she said.

"You smell like a party," he said.

"Oops!" She covered her mouth. "I think the punch was spiked."

"How much did you have?" her mother said.

"A cup," Finn said. She held up a finger. "Two cups." Another finger. "Three cups."

"Let me see how you look all dressed up." Her father whistled. "Knockout!"

"Come on, Daddy, tell the truth. Like my hair this way?" Finn shook her head like a girl in a shampoo ad.

"I'm telling you, baby, you look gorgeous."

"It's just my hair is down. And I'm wearing Mom's earrings."

"And Mom's blouse," her mother said.

"And Maggie's skirt," Finn added, laughing. She stopped herself too late. Mentioning Maggie's name had become a tricky thing, especially around her father.

"When'd you see your sister?" he said.

"Yesterday. Went over there to borrow her skirt."

He drummed his fingers on the table. "I said Finn could go," her mother put in.

Finn reached for the white pastry box on the table and snapped the string. "You guys act like Maggie committed an ax murder," she said, taking out a chocolate eclair. "What's so terrible about her living with Jim?"

Her father lit a cigarette. "You know how your mother and I feel. If Maggie wants to be married, that's one thing. This is nothing but shacking up."

Finn sighed and bit into one of the eclairs. Cream squirted into her mouth. "Yum," she said. "Did you bring them, Dad?"

"I did. Four for you, one for me, and one for Mom."

"Sounds fair," Finn said.

Her father took an eclair. "I'll just take a taste of yours, Ted," her mother said. "I'm on a diet."

"Nothing wrong with the way you are right now," her father said. "Eat a little more, Shirl, you'll only look better."

"Since you feel that way—" Finn's mother reached over and took his eclair.

They were all laughing. That was more like it. Finn hated it when her parents got gloomy about Maggie. She yawned.

"You can hardly keep your eyes open," her mother said.

Finn yawned again. "I should stay up all night," she said. "Remember the year Maggie and I did that?"

"I remember," her mother said. Her father started fiddling with the little radio on the cupboard.

"Guess I'll go to bed," Finn said. "Good night, everybody. Happy new year." In her room she dropped her clothes on the floor and fell into bed. She woke up a few hours later and began thinking about the party, the things she'd said, the things she'd done. She remembered laughing too loud, neighing like a fool, talking too fast. Then she remembered being on the bed with Jerry. Jerry? Who was he? What had that all been about? She felt hollow, empty, and lonely.

She lay on her back with her hands crossed over her chest and thought, Someday I'm going to die. It could happen any time. It could happen on the way to school. She thought of herself dead. Then of all the things she'd never know. She thought of never being in love, never having someone of her own. She pulled the covers up to her chin. Her parents had each other. Vida had Paul. Maggie had Jim. "I want someone, too," she said into the darkness.

4

The phone was ringing. Finn staggered down the hall to answer. The house was chilly. Her parents were still sleeping. She saw them curled up together as she passed their bedroom.

"Finn?" Maggie said. "Did I wake you?"

"Yes." Finn yawned. The radiators were clanking.

"We're driving to Auburn for the Polar Bear dip. Want to come?"

"What is it?" Finn said, pushing her hair off her face.

"You know, all those people who jump into Owasco Lake every year on the first of January. Jim's one of them. Are you up for the ride? Seth's coming," she added. Finn started to really wake up then. "Can you be ready in half an hour?" Maggie asked.

"I'll be waiting out front." Finn got dressed like lightning. Jeans, navy pea jacket, fur boots, a scarf tied behind her neck, and sunglasses for snow glare tucked in her pocket. On the way out she stopped at her parents' room and told her mother where she was going.

"Swimming in January?" her mother whispered. "Sounds weird."

"I know."

"Don't come home late. I bet you're tired from last night."

"I'm fine." She went outside, peeling a banana. She wasn't hungry, anyway. Jim's green VW bug came zipping around the corner. Maggie was driving. Finn crammed the last of the banana into her mouth and swallowed fast.

Maggie tapped the horn. Finn got in back next to Seth. "Hi," he said. His eyes were small and sleepy. A navy knit watch cap was pulled down over his dark hair. He looked terrific, but also older, and sort of aloof.

"Hi," Finn said and nervously stuck on her sunglasses.

"Great glasses," Maggie said, looking at her in the rearview mirror. Jim turned around to look. He was wearing a high fur cap, and with his curls and round face, he looked like a Russian cherub. "Very sophisticated," he said. "Where'd you get them, Finn?"

"Dad brought them home for me, from one of his trips. And a pair just like them for Mom." She was sorry as soon as she said it. How was Maggie supposed to feel? Finn was sure she'd hurt her sister's feelings. She yanked off the glasses and stuck them back in her pocket.

"So, Finn, how are you?" Jim said. "I hear you went partying last night. Did you have a good time?"

"Okay," she said. "Fine." She glanced at Seth. Sitting so close to him, she began worrying about her skin and her breath. She ran her tongue over her teeth, hoping her breath didn't smell of banana.

"You should have brought my skirt along," Maggie said. They were out of the city and on Route 5 now.

"I'm going to have it cleaned, Maggie. It got sort of crushed—" She broke off, thinking of Jerry.

"That must have been some wild party," her sister said. She and Jim laughed.

Seth smiled, but didn't say anything. What was he thinking? Did he think it was all kid stuff? Maybe he was just bored. As she thought this, he gave a really huge yawn.

" 'Scuse me," he said. "Last night was too much."

"Owasco Lake will clear your head," Jim said.

"I didn't know you were going in, too," Finn said. Seth nodded. Finn felt flustered. He hadn't said a word to her since she got in the car. Say nothing else, she ordered herself. But it was hard to sit so close to someone and not say something. He only had to turn his face, and they'd be kissing. Then he did turn and look at her. Her hands got damp.

"I like your sweater," she blurted. He was wearing a hand-knit blue sweater with reindeer around the border.

"A friend knit it for me."

A girl, Finn thought. "Toby?" Seth shook his head. Why had she said Toby? There were probably dozens of girls dying to knit him sweaters and socks and scarves and anything else he wanted.

Up front Maggie and Jim were singing. "You have

very pretty eyes," Seth said. "Blue-green, like the sea. Nice."

He liked her eyes! Instead of saying thank you, she got rattled and stuck on her sunglasses again. Oh, what a fool! Now she ordered herself to say something, *quick*! "Do you go in Polar Bear swimming every year?"

"This will be the first time," Seth said. "Jim's the real Polar Bear. Don't you want to know why I'm doing it?"

"Yes." She snatched off the sunglasses and smiled at him.

"Well," he said, smiling back at her, "My brother challenged me, and I accepted. Apparently all you need are nerves of iron and a skin like a rhino."

At Owasco Outlet Maggie parked and they walked toward a building, where the boys changed.

Maggie was carrying a couple of big yellow towels.

"All we need is a picnic basket," Finn said, stamping her feet to keep them warm.

"Right," Maggie said. "And the beach umbrella."

"Suntan lotion." Finn's breath puffed into the air.

"You've got the sunglasses." Maggie wrapped her arms around herself. "Isn't this crazy? I don't actually believe the guys are going to go through with it."

When Seth and Jim emerged in their bathing trunks, Finn thought they looked like fighters ready to go into training. Except, she noticed, Jim had a little pot belly, while beautiful Seth was really . . . beautiful! His arms and legs were muscular, and his chest was covered with a faint fuzz of dark hair.

"Are you freezing?" Maggie cried, rubbing Jim's back.

"Not yet, not yet," he said. He jogged toward the pier with Maggie.

"Wish me luck," Seth said to Finn. There were goose pimples on his arms.

"I do!" Impulsively, she pulled off a silver and turquoise ring she wore on her middle finger. "My good-luck ring," she said, holding it out. "Wear it."

He looked at her, then took the ring. "Thanks." He put it on his little finger.

A man with a TV camera perched on his shoulder called, "Polar Bears! Get into three rows, please, for pictures."

"We're at the edge of Owasco Lake, ladies and gentlemen," a woman with a mike said into a tape machine. "The temperature is a brisk sixteen degrees above zero, and the sun is shining. A fine day for a swim, if you happen to be a Polar Bear."

The Polar Bears jostled one another toward the end of the pier. A big uneven hole had been chopped in the ice. The water looked black. A chunky woman in a polka-dot suit was the first to jump in. "Oh, Lord," she cried as she surfaced. "It's so fine!" Her teeth were chattering.

Finn stuck her hands into her pockets. She felt like a coward compared to the Polar Bears. Just watching them made her cold.

"And a one, and a two, and a three," the crowd sang. A man jumped. As he hit the water, everyone groaned. "Oooohhh!" Then another man jumped in, holding his nose. "Ooooohhhhh!"

Finn watched Seth, whose shoulders were hunched against the cold. More people were going in. She grabbed Maggie's arm. "Jim's getting ready!"

Jim stood poised, then dove in cleanly. Water

splashed up. "Oh!" Finn cried, hanging on Maggie. "I don't believe it." Then Seth dove in. A chunk of ice bobbed in his wake. He swam a few vigorous strokes behind Jim, turned, and swam rapidly back to the pier. He climbed out.

"Jesus," he said, grabbing the towel from Maggie. He looked so stunned, Finn felt sorry for him.

Jim came out, his skin as red as if it had been burned. "That was great!" He slapped his chest.

"Why'd you come out so soon?" Seth said, starting for the dressing building.

On the way back to Syracuse Maggie said they were going to have breakfast at the apartment. "Can you guys hold out?" Maggie said. "You must be hungry as wolves after that swim."

"We guys can do anything," Jim said. He was driving. "You name it, we can do it."

"Ego, ego," Maggie said. "All because of a little plunge into cold water. Going to do it again next year, Seth?"

"You'll have to tie me up and throw me in."

"It was a change from the hot water you're usually in," Jim needled.

Seth ignored him. "What a schmucky thing to do," he murmured to Finn. "Here's your ring. Good thing I had it, or I might have sunk to the bottom and never come up again." He groaned. "I hate it when I do things without thinking."

"I know what you mean," she said sympathetically. "It's that Was-it-really-me? after-the-party feeling."

"Right, right. Well, that'll teach me to try and outdo

my brother. I thought I learned that lesson a long time ago." He was talking in a low voice, only for Finn's ears.

"What are you two whispering about back there?" Maggie said.

"I'm telling Finn all the things I've done." Seth smiled conspiratorially at Finn. "Farm work," he said louder, counting off on his fingers. "Construction. Truck driver, dishwasher, short-order cook—"

"Jackass work," Jim interrupted. "You've been muddling around for three years. You haven't gotten started on anything."

"I've been learning about life," Seth said.

Jim made a derisive noise. Seth jutted out his chin and gave Jim the finger. He and Finn looked at each other. "I don't blame you," Finn whispered, leaning toward Seth.

Jim hadn't seen the gesture. "You know," he said, "right now if you told Dad you wanted to go back to school, he'd be behind you one hundred percent. You've got the brains for college. You're just wasting yourself."

The car hummed over the road. There was snow everywhere, bare trees, long empty fields with yellow grass frozen above the snow.

"I'm impressed with all your jobs," Finn said. "I'd like to do a lot of things, too, some day."

"The experience is good," Seth said. "I believe in girls doing everything, too."

"Which job did you like best?"

"Farming, definitely. I'm going to get a job here, save my money, then buy land in Maine, where I hear it's still pretty cheap. Or maybe Vancouver. See if I can farm, be self-sufficient. That's my master plan."

"That's really interesting," Finn said.

"Nobody in my family thinks so," Seth said with a half laugh.

In Maggie's apartment they made scrambled eggs and sausage, toast, and coffee. They were all starved by then. After they ate and cleaned up, Jim went to sleep on the couch with his head in Maggie's lap. Seth got out the checkerboard.

"Want to play?" he said to Finn. He set the board on the floor and they sat down across from each other.

"I warn you," she said. "I play to win. No mercy given."

Outside it had started to snow again. The game got down to three of Seth's kings and three of Finn's. Maggie had dropped her book and put her head back. Seth and Finn were keeping their voices low.

Finn made a stupid mistake, and Seth jumped two of her kings. "You didn't want to win," he said. "Not in your heart of hearts."

"You're right. I love to lose." She picked up the board and dumped it on his head.

"Oh-ho, you want to play dirty!" He threw checkers at her.

"A checker war!" Finn scooped up checkers.

Maggie opened her eyes. "Hey, you two!"

"Your sister is vicious," Seth said, and leaning over, he rumpled Finn's hair.

Last night Jerry, Finn thought. Today—Seth. She must be doing something right.

5

"Girls, girls," Miss Moran, the physical ed teacher called. "I know it's only the first day after vacation— and that you all ate too much—" Groans. "—and in some cases drank too much—" Snickers. "—but I find it hard to believe you have all lost the use of your limbs. This hasn't been a volleyball game. This has been a disaster!"

Vida poked Finn. "She means me." Vida hated gym.

"I don't know what to say about those who don't make the slightest effort," Miss Moran went on, tossing her long, dark ponytail over her shoulder. "This is supposed to be a physical ed class."

"Miss Moran," Finn said, "how about the physical dead class?"

Nancy Govenda tapped Finn's shoulder. "A very witty remark. Where'd you hear it?"

"I didn't. I made it up."

Nancy smiled disbelievingly. She was a short, sturdy girl who was always trying to get under Finn's skin.

Later the girls crowded down the stairs to the locker room. Finn and Vida got in line for the showers. "Where were you New Year's Day," Vida said. "I called, and your father said you were out."

"I went to Auburn with Maggie, Jim, and Seth."

"Who's Seth?"

"Jim's brother. Remember?"

"Oh, Jim's *brother*. The yummy one."

"Right." Finn told Vida about the Polar Bears. Vida shook her head. "I don't get it. Are they crazy?"

Nancy, who was standing ahead of Vida, turned. "You have to understand their psychology, Vida. They're middle-aged men trying to act young. They have youth complexes."

"They're not all middle-aged, and some of them are women," Finn said.

"I'm sure the majority are middle-aged," Nancy said. "They may have deep inferiority feelings. They're trying to compensate."

"Nancy, are you taking that psychology mini-course?"

"Yes, and it's fascinating." Nancy stepped into a vacated shower and adjusted the faucets.

"Vida, I think he likes me," Finn said.

"Who?"

"Seth. Pay attention."

"I thought he was old," Vida said.

Finn leaned on Vida's shoulder. "Nineteen," she said, tossing it out casually.

"Nineteen," Vida yelped. "Finn Rousseau! How'd you manage that?"

"Nothing to it." Then she couldn't keep up her casual pose. She thumped Vida on the back. "He likes me, Vida. I'm sure of it."

"Well, what happpened?"

"Nothing, really. What'd you expect to happen? I just met the guy."

Vida nodded. "Oh, I forgot to ask you. How'd you make out with Jerry?"

Finn grinned. From the corner of her eye she saw Nancy watching. "We made out just fine. First he asked me to go with him, and then—"

"Wait, wait," Vida interrupted. "Jerry asked you to go with him?" Finn nodded. "And you're talking about some other guy who's not even real? *Nineteen.* He's too old for you. Is he in college?"

"Nooo," Finn said. "I told you, he works." She didn't want to tell Vida Seth was a high school dropout. She'd think that was a black mark against his character.

"What does his age matter? It's what sort of person —God, Vida, he's gorgeous. Dark hair, high cheekbones —you should have seen him in his swimming trunks."

"Is this for real?" Nancy said, stepping out of the shower. She tucked her towel around her waist. She was the only one who showed off that way. "Sounds like wish fulfillment to me."

"Oh, he's for real," Finn said.

"Well, you know how it is, Finn," Nancy said sweetly. "Some people, if they can't have what they want, they make it up. Then after a while it seems real."

Finn and Vida looked at each other. "Nancy, Seth ain't no fantasy," Finn said.

Nancy put on her flannel shirt, carefully rolling up

the sleeves. "Fantasy is nothing to be ashamed of, Finn. Everyone does it sometimes."

"Seth is real," Finn said. "As real as this finger." She stuck her middle finger up in the air.

Walking out of the locker room, Vida said to her, "What are you going to do about Jerry?"

"Nothing, probably."

"I was hoping you two would hit it off. Then you and Jerry and Paul and I could do things together. It would be a lot of fun."

"I know," Finn said.

"And you're not really serious about Seth, anyway."

"Vida, I like him an awful lot. I really do."

"But Finn, these older guys want sex. Are you ready for that?"

"You know how I feel."

"You better stay clear of him, then."

"Vida," Finn said, "don't you think Jerry's got the same thing on his mind?"

"At least we know Jerry."

"Well, Seth is Jim's brother, and Jim is practically my brother-in-law. Anyway, it doesn't matter. Jerry or Seth, I'm not doing anything I don't want to."

When Finn left school, it was snowing. Vida had gone off with Paul who said he'd heard that Jerry was sick. Finn scuffed along, sticking out her tongue for a taste of snow. All that talk about Seth! She felt a little foolish. When you got down to it, what had gone on between them? A game of checkers. That was it. And she had built him up, built up the way he felt about her, as if she really knew. Nancy was right. Wish fulfillment!

A green VW bug came around the corner. Finn's

stomach jerked. It was Jim's car, and Seth was driving. He must be looking for her! She stepped into the road and waved. "Seth!"

He stopped. "Seth, it's me." Finally he rolled down the window. "Oh, hello." Finn had the sick feeling that he'd forgotten her name. She felt like diving into the nearest snowbank and never coming up.

"Hi, Roussey." She turned to see Nancy Govenda crossing the street toward her. Oh, no. Not Nancy. Not now.

Nancy's eyes darted to Seth in the VW, to Finn, then back to Seth. Finn could almost see the wheels whirring and the gears clicking. So there really *is* a Seth! Here was the living proof. Handsome Seth in his reindeer sweater and long, dark hair, on their very own school corner.

Nancy became an instant believer. She leaned into the opened window. "You must be Seth. I've heard all about you."

Finn slid into the VW next to Seth, rolled up the window, and said, "Drive me home?" All she wanted was to get away from Nancy. Fast. "Spring Street. Do you know where it is?" She gave him directions.

Seth nodded and drove. He didn't say anything. Oh, God. What had she done? Obviously he hadn't come looking for her at all. Pure coincidence that he'd been driving by. She had made something out of nothing. She was crazy. She thought of all the things she'd told Vida that Nancy had overheard. *He likes me, he likes me . . .* She winced, hearing her own excited voice. She was a fool. No, that was too kind. She was an idiot.

She glanced at him. He really was beautiful. It made

her throat ache to look at him. She didn't know what it was exactly. His hair . . . the way he held himself . . . oh, everything. Just perfect. And perfectly indifferent to her. That little frown on his face. Was he still trying to remember her name? Vida had told her—he was too old for her. He wasn't interested. The other day—that had just been being nice to Maggie's little sister.

He turned the corner onto Spring Street. "Third house from the corner," Finn said. "The one with the porch. We live upstairs." She didn't have to say that. *Shut up. Nobody's interested.*

He pulled up in front of the house. "Well, thanks," she said. She reached for the door, and as she did she heard herself saying, "Do you remember my name now?"

"What?" he said.

"My *name*."

"Finn. Are you kidding? Why should I forget your name?"

She was horrified. "Oh, I don't know. Forget I said it!"

"I don't understand," he said.

"It was the way you looked at me when you drove up. As if you didn't know me."

"I'm really sorry. I've been looking for work, and I'm feeling sort of down. I hate looking for work and being turned down."

She'd misjudged everything. She felt worse than ever. He had serious things on his mind, and she'd been acting like a nit. "Good-bye," she mumbled. "Thanks for the ride."

"Finn—"

But she was already out of the car. She slid on an icy patch, caught herself, saw him staring at her, looking baffled. Her face flamed. She rushed up on the porch, pulling out her house key. She stood there, head down, fumbling with it. Inside she dropped her books and turned to look out the little side window. He was gone. She had felt so crazy with humiliation, she hadn't even heard him drive away.

6

On Monday a snowstorm closed down the city and the schools didn't open. Finn's mother couldn't get into work, and she and Finn's father, who'd been home for a week this time, bundled up and went walking. Finn stayed in bed late thinking about Seth. No, not really. If she truly thought about him, she wanted to kill herself. But if she let her imagination roam, that was different. She spread her hair out on the pillow, and imagined him bending over her, whispering her name. *Finn . . . Finn . . . you have beautiful eyes . . . beautiful hair . . . I like you . . . no, I love you. . . . I love your hair, let me touch your hair. . . .*

Finn ate breakfast in her favorite bathrobe, a splendid green-and-gold affair with peacocks that had been Maggie's. Snow days always made her feel holidayish. She wandered around the kitchen nibbling toast and jelly and thinking vaguely of what she'd do today. The windows were dotted with little clumps of snow. In the backyard snow clung thickly to the blue spruce.

When she went outside later, the wind had died down. She plowed through knee-high drifts into the road then followed a single set of tire tracks. The whole world was covered by a fresh white blanket that sparkled brilliantly in the sun. She put on her sunglasses.

All around her she heard the scrape of shovels. Voices carried far in the unusually still air. From Salina Street came the heavy rumbling of the plows. A woman on skis passed her, then a boy hauling a younger child on a sled. The child was bundled up so that only two shiny eyes showed.

At an Italian bakery she bought a hot pointed loaf. "You got into work today," she said. The white-aproned, floury-looking man laughed. "Never got out. Been here since last night."

She kept walking in the cold air, nibbling the hot bread. Walking and eating and looking, she was more than halfway to Maggie's before she realized that was where she was going.

In front of Maggie's building she scattered the crumbs of the bread for the birds. She looked up at Maggie's window. She could go up, but what if Seth was there? She'd say, Hi, Seth. And he'd say, Hi, birdbrain!

Suddenly she felt he was at the window, looking down. She ducked her head and ran, not stopping till she was around the corner.

At home her father was at the stove in his shirt-sleeves stirring a pot of tomato sauce. "I just walked six miles," Finn said.

"Atta baby," her father said. "You kids are all right."

Her mother was watching TV. "Where'd you go, honey?"

"Just for a walk," Finn said. The phone rang and she picked it up. It was Hurley, the dispatcher at Roadway.

"That you, Finn? Tell your dad he's on the board for tomorrow morning. Houston."

"What time?" Finn said.

"Eight o'clock."

"He'll be there." She hung up.

"Hurley?" her father said. Finn nodded. "About time," her father said.

"Oh, you and your itchy feet," her mother said. "You had a big six days at home. Another six wouldn't have bothered me."

"You're just saying that because it's true." Her father winked at Finn. "You adore me. I don't blame you. Handsome devil like me."

The next day when Finn got up, her mother was in the kitchen cooking breakfast. The shower was running. "You mind Dad's going away?" Finn said. She peeled an orange, looking out the window. There was a white crust of snow like a cake-icing on the Barnowskis' roof.

"I like it better when he's home," her mother said, putting a scrambled egg in front of Finn. "I keep wishing they'd give him some jobs around here."

Her father came into the kitchen. His hair was wet from the shower. He was wearing the dark green Pendleton shirt Finn and Maggie had bought him last year for his birthday.

"Finn, your egg is getting cold," her mother said.

"I'm not hungry." Finn sighed. She should have gone up to Maggie's yesterday. If Seth had been there, she could have talked to him, wiped out the horrible impression she'd left the day he drove her home from school.

"Well, eat a little," her mother urged.

Shaking her head, Finn pushed back her chair. "I'm really not hungry. I'm going to school."

She kissed her father. "Good luck, Dad. Have a good trip." They never said good-bye, just—good luck.

"I'll bring you back something."

"You don't have to. Just drive safe."

Outside the air was bitterly cold. Finn's eyes teared. Her cheeks froze. It was wonderful to get into the warm school. First period there was a special assembly. Someone from the Historical Society was going to speak on "Winter in Central New York One Hundred Years Ago."

"What can he say? It was cold," Finn said, sitting down next to Vida, who was holding hands with Paul.

Paul smiled at her. "You're looking nice, Finn." He had a big, unruly head of hair.

"What'd you guys do yesterday?" Finn said.

"We went skiing," Vida started. Then she raised her hand. "Jerry. Over here." Jerry, looking spiffy in a thick, white cableknit sweater, joined them. "Sit down right here next to Finn," Vida said.

It was the first time Finn had seen Jerry since the party. "Heard you were sick, Jerry."

"Miss me? Today's my first day out of the house. I had viral pneumonia."

"That sounds serious," Finn said. "Are you all right now?"

"In the important areas, I'm A-okay." He gave her The Look.

Vida leaned across Finn. "We've been talking about you, Jerry. Finn and I," she said pointedly.

Paul gave his big laugh. "Jerry, you got all the girls worried."

"Well, we missed Jerry," Vida said. "Didn't we, Finn?"

Finn gave Vida a Look of her own. Talk about laying it on with a shovel! Between Vida and Jerry she could feel strings being drawn over her, little nets being thrown, tugging her nearer and nearer to Jerry. As if he were the fisherman, and she a big, indolent fish.

On the stage the principal rapped for attention. "Students and teachers, may I have your attention, please."

Jerry took one of Finn's fingers and shook it lightly. "I want to ask you something. Is there someone you like?"

"Where?" she whispered. "You mean in school?"

"Anywhere."

"Not really."

"Are you sure? How about that guy in the green bug?"

Finn stared at him in amazement. "How do you know about that?"

"I've got my spies hard at work," Jerry said, looking pleased with the effect of his question. "Nancy Govenda and I came into school together this morning."

"Jesus," Finn muttered.

"Nancy said you were pretty hot about this guy in the green car. Any competition there?"

On stage the speaker was being introduced. Finn lowered her voice. "He's just a guy I met a few times."

They were sunk low in their seats, talking behind their hands. "I take it I've still got a chance," Jerry said, moving so his shoulder touched hers. "I like tall—"

"I know, I know," Finn whispered. "Tall girls with minds of their own."

"What about you? What do you like?"

"Well . . ." How were these things pinned down? How could you catch your feelings and label them? Take Seth. He was so handsome . . . and so superior! So sweet . . . and so patronizing! *Forget Seth*, she told herself. *You don't have anything in common!* He was nineteen, she was fifteen. He was a dropout, she was a schoolgirl. He was male, she was female. North Pole and South Pole!

"Remember what we talked about at Cindy's party?" Jerry said, leaning toward her. Finn had the feeling that the more she hesitated, the more interested Jerry became. She ought to just tell him, No use, Jerry. Give up. Then she thought of herself walking through the halls with Jerry. Jerry and Finn. Nancy Govenda would know. Everybody would know. She would suddenly be in the social swing. Vida would be pleased. She could stop thinking about Seth. Her mind flapped like a sheet in the breeze. Yes. No. This way, that way.

"The offer's still open," Jerry said. Even in an assembly hall full of people he managed the Great Jerry Turn-on. And even without the punch it was effective. Finn felt her skin warming.

"Thanks," she said.

"Let me know," he said. "You call me. I won't call you." She nodded. Fair enough.

That night she was asleep when the phone rang. She was dreaming . . . pedaling down a steep hill. Someone was at the foot of the hill . . . Oh, let me get there! she thought, waking up in confusion.

The phone! She scrambled barefoot through the darkened hall. "Seth?" she blurted.

"Francie?" a man's voice answered.

"What?"

"This Francie?"

"No, it's Finn."

"Oh, guess I have the wrong number. You have a nice voice. What do you look like, Finn?"

She banged down the phone. "Creep."

Moments later, pulling the covers over her shoulders, she realized why she'd said Seth's name. Her dream had been about him. She'd been biking down the hill, flying free. And Seth had been waiting for her at the bottom of the hill.

7

"Conducts secret desperate affair with actress many years younger than himself," Finn copied into her notebook from *Brief Lives*. It was Saturday. She was in the library downtown researching Charles Dickens.

"Ellen Ternan . . . actress . . ." she wrote. She leaned on her elbow. Where had the lovers gone when they wanted to be together? She imagined them hurrying down a dark, foggy London street, hand in hand, looking worriedly over their shoulders, then ducking into a doorway and embracing. Were they desperate because he was so much older than she was?

Reaching into the white paper bag at her side, Finn took out a handful of peanuts. Almost two weeks since she'd met him and she was still thinking about Seth. But he wasn't thinking about her. Finn chewed a peanut ferociously and reached for another one. The shells crackled. At the table ahead of her a woman turned and stared sternly. She had a round pretty face beneath gray hair pinned into a big loose knot.

Finn dropped her eyes. "The readings of his works in public brought him a new career, a new fortune . . ."

She scanned the rest of the long paragraph looking for more juicy stuff about Charlie's secret, desperate affair with Ellen. How much younger was Ellen? The book didn't say. Ten years younger? Six years younger? Four years? Was four "many years younger"?

What if she could be in the car with Seth again? Everything would be different. He'd drive her home. She'd talk intelligently. Amusingly. Seriously. At her house, she'd say, *Thanks for the ride. My pleasure*, he'd say. He'd lean toward her and kiss her.

Finn, I'm so crazy about you . . . I never knew a girl like you. . . . And he'd kiss her again . . . and again . . .

She scraped back her chair. It wasn't going to happen. Not that way. Not any way. And if it ever did, somehow, it would be just kiss and run. He'd leave the scene of the accident without a backward glance. *The victim was found wandering in a dazed condition. For weeks she has not said a single intelligible word. The police are still hunting for the perpetrator of this foul crime.*

FOUL CRIME, she wrote in her notebook. Then, doodling, she substituted the *l* from *foul* for the *r* from *crime* and wrote FOUR CLIME. She studied the words as if they meant something. FOUR. Aha. A clue. Four letters in Seth's name. Four letters in her name. Four years difference in their ages.

It was unFOURtunate that FOUR girls who FOURtified themselves with FOURteen FOURtune cookies should FOURfeit their FOURmidable—

"Their formidable—" She mumbled. She bent over the paper, then another word entered her mind. FOURnicate.

No, come on, do your work. She read sternly through the weighty sentences, looking for stuff she could use. She yawned. FOURce yourself to work.

Someone touched her on the shoulder. "I thought that was you," Seth said, smiling down at her. Finn stared. Had she conjured him up? She put out her hand, then drew it quickly back. She could feel a smile spreading over her face.

"What are you doing here?" she said.

"Same thing you are, I suppose."

"I'm studying."

"I'm looking for something good to read." He dropped into the seat opposite her. "Read any good books lately?"

"*Wuthering Heights,*" she said, staring at him.

"Read it a long time ago. What are you studying?"

"Something for English. Dickens." He looked wonderful. Too wonderful to be a mirage—faded jeans, boots, blue denim work shirt, sheepskin jacket over his shoulder.

He studied her across the table. "How are you?" he said. His eyes on her face were warm. She felt confused. "Have a peanut," she said, pushing the bag toward him.

He reached for her book. "Good old *Brief Lives.* Like it?"

She shook her head. "Bo-ring."

"How about *Bartlett's?* It's a book of indexed quotations from famous people. Let's say you wanted to find some good pithy remarks about love—"

"Love," she repeated, although she knew perfectly well about *Bartlett's*.

"Look up *love* in the index and then you find—"

"I know," she said, breaking through her trance. "Everyone knows about *Bartlett's*." Suddenly she got mad. What did he think she was? A know-nothing? A dumb, jerky adolescent goof that he could ignore or lecture as the mood suited him?

"I used to look up quotes from Big *B's* and drop them casually into conversation," Seth said. "Pretty funny, now that I think of it."

"It sounds obnoxious to me," Finn said. She regretted it immediately. She had meant to sound cool and mature. Instead she just sounded snippy. "I'm sorry," she said. "That was rude of me."

"No, you were right," he said. "It was obnoxious."

"No, really, I didn't mean it," she insisted.

"You were still right."

She stared at him. That wasn't arrogant. Or superior. Who was he? It came over her that she really didn't know him. That up to this moment she had only been dazzled by his looks.

He leaned toward her. "Remember the day I gave you a ride home?" She nodded. "You must be good luck. Right after I left you, I stopped for a cup of coffee, asked the manager if he needed anyone, and got a job."

"That's great," she said. "Where is it?"

"Apple Cafeteria over on Onondaga Street. Know it?"

"Congratulations," Finn said. She slid the bag of peanuts toward him. "Have some more. Celebrate. But don't chew too loud." She pointed to the woman ahead of her.

He slid his chair closer to hers. "This job is okay," he said. "I ought to make some money. I've been working overtime all week."

"How terrible," Finn said. "I mean, wonderful that you're making so much money." She was starting to feel really good. Her smile was brilliant.

"Well, at least my master plan is in operation," he said.

"Terrific." Master Plan? She remembered something of the sort, but the details had escaped her.

"I've been trying to figure out how much money I'll need."

"Good idea." How much money for what? To buy a car? Take a sea voyage?

"Couple thou should get me started."

"Certainly should," she agreed wisely. Give me a hint . . . just a little hint . . .

"I've been reading about Maine—"

A chink of light entered the darkness. Maine . . . land . . . *farming* . . . "Farming!" she exclaimed. Then at his surprised look, she added quickly, "I don't know anything about farming."

"Well . . . " He smiled. "Who knows? Maybe I'll find out I don't know as much as I think, either." He looked over at the clock. "I've really got to go." But he didn't move. Instead he put his hand over hers and moved his thumb back and forth across her wrist.

She stared at his hand, hypnotized with delight. He was saying something. She focused on the words. ". . . Friday night off. We could go to a movie."

"Friday night," she repeated.

"Okay. Great. Pick you up about seven." He stood up, pulling on his jacket, tipping his hat down over his eyes. She watched him walk out. The moment he was through the door, she burst out of her seat, slinging her things together, smiling uncontrollably at the gray-haired woman.

"It's a fantastic day outside," Finn said to her. "I mean, it's cold, but it's fantastic!" She couldn't stop smiling. "Don't sit in here all day and study," she said. "It's too fantastic outside!"

"Yes, it's beautiful out," the woman said. She pushed a pencil into her slipping knot of hair. "You're right." And she smiled at Finn as if she knew of Finn's happiness, and approved, and was giving her blessing.

8

Sliding around the kitchen in her red wool slipper-socks, Finn flipped a grapefruit in the air, caught it, rolled it onto the table, then juggled two eggs on her way from the fridge to the stove. Such were her powers on this day, The Day After The Day That Seth Asked Her Out, that there was nary a slip between hand and egg. She deposited both eggs, shaken but unbroken, into a pan of water, and turned over the egg timer. Then she just stood there watching the water bubble up around the eggs and thinking about the way she was going to ask her mother's permission to go out with Seth Friday night.

Ordinarily she never beat around the bush when she wanted to go someplace, or see someone. But this time, no matter how she thought of putting it, it came out wrong. *There's this boy I met in the library. . . . You know, Jim has a brother, and he asked me. . . . Okay if I go to the movies Friday? No, not with Vida. . . .*

Why did it seem so difficult? Just say it! she told herself.

She was measuring coffee into the basket when her mother appeared. "Sit down," Finn said, "I'm doing everything." She set her mother's place, popped bread into the toaster, and cut the grapefruit in half.

"What's this all about?" Her mother was dressed for work and had the fat Sunday newspaper under her arm.

"Surprise, surprise." Finn turned on the fire under the coffee. "Ask not what you can do for your daughter, ask what your daughter can do for you."

"Gladly, but why?" her mother said.

Because I want you to say yes when I ask about Friday night. She fished out the eggs. "Here you are, madam, two perfectly done three-minute eggs."

"Thanks, honey," her mother said, glancing at the newspaper.

"I'm also cleaning my room today."

"The pigpen?"

"It's only a pigpen by your standards. I call it cozy."

Her mother shuddered. "Sweetie, I pity your husband."

"Mom, you're so neat, you're practically compulsive." In her mother's room there was never anything in sight. Everything was tucked away in drawers and closets, and even the drawers and closets were marvels of neatness.

"I just like things in their place," her mother said, tapping open an egg. "Oh, Finn, it's sort of underdone."

"I did it three minutes."

"Was the water boiling? The water has to be boiling

when you put in the egg." Her mother stirred her spoon around in the egg, then took a bite of toast. "Oh!" She jumped up and snatched the coffeepot off the burner just as it boiled over.

Finn groaned. Finn, the little household helper.

"You want one of these eggs?" her mother said.

"Ugh, no thanks, I like mine almost hard-boiled."

Her mother laughed. "Good thing I don't." She drank her coffee, then said, "I'd better get going." She yawned. "Working on Sunday is a nuisance. For some reason I never feel really wide awake." She stood up. "That was really nice, honey."

Now's the time, Finn said to herself. Just ask her if it's okay if you go to a movie on Friday night with a friend.

"Are you really going to clean up your room?" her mother said. "That's good news. But what's the bad news?" She was smiling.

Finn laughed, but as she did all the bad news filled her mind. *Flash* . . . 19-YEAR-OLD BROTHER OF SISTER'S LIVE-IN BOYFRIEND ASKS FOR DATE. OUTRAGED MOTHER STRANGLES DAUGHTER. Now Finn understood why she hadn't just asked straight out. Seth was different. Seth was nineteen. Seth was Jim's brother, and Finn knew those two things were going to make all the difference in the world to her mother.

Late in the afternoon she called Maggie. "I want to ask you something." She leaned on the cupboard, the phone clamped to her ear. "Someone asked me to go to a movie—"

"So?" Maggie said. "I was dating when I was fifteen."

"It's not just any boy," Finn said. "It's Seth."

"You're kidding me."

Finn was a little offended by her sister's surprise, but she went on, "I'm afraid Mom won't let me because he's Jim's brother."

"Oh, I don't know, Finn," Maggie said. "That's so backward! Guilt by association? Seth's a real nice guy. I don't see why Mom should object to him."

"They don't even like it when I go to visit you."

"They don't have to like it. They only have to let you. Just ask. I'd put in a word for you, but right now my influence at home is zero minus."

That call wasn't worth much, Finn thought, hanging up. But what had she expected? She didn't actually know. It had been more of a reflex than a thought-out action—just running to Maggie for a little help when times got tough. She thought she'd say something to her mother that evening when she got back from work, but she didn't get around to it. Still, it was okay. She was flying high. Tuesday afternoon when they played basketball she was all over the court, dunking the ball into the basket and making incredible passes. She felt powerful. As if she could do anything, even make Seth fall in love with her.

The odd thing was, she didn't tell Vida. She hugged Seth's invitation to herself, like some precious secret. She'd always shared things with Vida. I'll tell her, she kept thinking, and didn't. In the same way she kept putting off asking her mother. There was never the exact right moment. Then, incredibly, it was Wednesday and she still hadn't said anything.

After supper she cleared the table, gearing up again. Strange how the longer you waited to do something, the harder it got. At this rate Seth would be at the door Friday night, and she'd still be trying to find the right moment and the right words.

Her mother was going to the Mall. A sale on shoes. "Wonderful," Finn said quickly, "I'll go with you."

"Don't tell me your feet have grown again."

"No problem, no problem, I'll just keep you company." She'd say it on the drive. *By the way, someone asked me to a movie Friday night. Okay?* And her mother, concentrating on the driving, would say, *Sure. Why not?* Simple.

But all the way to the Mall Finn sat silently. Not a squeak out of her.

In the Mall she waved to Paul, who was working in Valdone's Cheese 'n Coffee Shop. She helped her mother pick out a pair of brown suede platforms. She bought herself a pair of socks. When they left, it was snowing again, and the roads were slippery. Her mother drove slowly. *Do it!* Finn told herself. *Now.*

"Mom . . ." She cleared her throat, took a deep breath and said fast, "I have something to ask you. There's this—uh—boy—" She stumbled, and then heard herself blurting out the whole thing in the worst possible way. "Jim's brother asked me to go to the movies Friday night."

Her mother peered through the windshield. "Jim's *brother*? Where'd he come from?"

"Auburn."

"What's he doing here?"

"Visiting Jim."

"Doesn't he go to school?"

"No," Finn said, sinking down into the seat.

"Why?"

"He dropped out." Worse and worse. She stared at the little half-moons of clear window made by the windshield wipers. Click-clack . . . click-clack . . . you blew it . . . you blew it . . . click-clack . . . click-clack . . .

"How old is he?"

"Nineteen."

"What?" Her mother glanced at her. "No, Finn. Forget it."

"Why?" She bolted up in the seat. "Because he's Jim's brother?" She didn't wait for an answer. "That's guilt by association."

"Yes, because he's Jim's brother. And what's more, he's four years older than you. And something else—I'm sure he's drawn certain conclusions about you because of the way Maggie is living."

"Mom, no, that's so stupid. You don't even know him."

"I don't want to know him, Finn." The light changed, and the car jolted forward.

"Jesus! You're so unfair."

"Life's not fair," her mother said. "Look at what Maggie did—is that fair to me and your father?"

"Lots of people don't get married."

"I don't care about lots of people. I care about my own daughters. There's Maggie, with Jim. And now here comes his brother, interested in you. Oh, no, Finn, oh, no!"

"Mom, I only want to go to the movies with him. I don't want to move in with him!"

"No," her mother said. "No, Finn. No, no, no."

"Why? Just tell me *why*. Just give me one reason I can respect, instead of a bunch of emotional shit."

"Finnis!" The car slued sideways as her mother made a fast turn onto their block. She wrenched the wheel around. They skidded down the snowy street, then came to a crunching halt in front of their driveway. Before her mother could back up, the car stalled.

"Oh, hell!" her mother exclaimed.

"It's just a movie," Finn said. "Jesus, Mom—"

"Shut up!"

Hatred for her mother swelled her throat. You bitch, Finn thought, you old bitch! She leaped out of the car, slamming the door, and ran into the house. She went to her room and slammed that door. I knew it, she thought. I knew it, I knew it, I knew it!

9

The next morning Finn didn't speak to her mother. She went through the day in a state of submerged misery. She just wanted to be left alone. But the moment her mother walked in from work that night, she started on Finn. "I thought you were going to clean up the kitchen. You haven't done a thing."

Finn followed her mother's glance around the kitchen. "Okay, okay!" She turned on the hot tap full force, grabbed the detergent and poured it in. Water sloshed onto the floor.

"Finn," her mother said, "you're pushing me."

Finn glared. Pushing *her*. It was incredible how her mother managed to turn everything around.

"I'm going to take a hot tub," her mother said. "My feet are like ice. Don't forget to put on the potatoes."

Finn scrubbed the potatoes, banged them into the

baker, and turned up the fire. Too high. Who cared! She swallowed hard.

From the bathroom, her mother called, "Finn? Any mail?"

"Postcard," she said. Her father had mailed it from Houston. " 'Good to get out of the snow. Wish you were here. Love, Daddy.' "

"From your father?" her mother called.

"Yesss."

"Let me see it!"

"What?" Finn called back, deliberately obtuse.

"Let me see it."

Finn stuck her head in the bathroom door. "He didn't send it to you."

Her mother was soaping her arms. She looked up. "What did he write—something I can't read, but the mailman can?"

"You never let me see the letters he writes you!" Childish, but she was mad.

"That's different," her mother said. "This is just a postcard."

"It's always different when it's you," Finn said. "One set of rules for you. Right? And another for me."

Her mother pulled the plug on the tub with her toe and stood up. "I don't know what's the matter with you, Finn . . ." Naked, she was grand and imposing, like some wonderful painting. Finn had the terrible feeling that she would never be as beautiful as her mother. Without replying, she ran out of the bathroom, grabbed her jacket, and went outside for a long walk.

In the morning her mother waited to drive Finn to

school. "I want to talk to you." Finn stood near the car. Clouds of exhaust poisoned the air. "Get in," her mother said.

Finn put her books on the seat between her and her mother. She looked out the window. If her mother wanted to talk, let her talk. She didn't have anything to say.

"Look," her mother said, driving slowly, "I know you're upset about the other night. Our talk about Jim's brother. I want you to understand that I'm not keeping you from seeing him to hurt you. I thought you understood that. I'm older and I look at things differently. I have—well, call it wisdom, you don't have."

Like hell I'll call it wisdom. Finn stared out the frosty window.

"Finn, are you listening?" Finn didn't turn her head. Her mother sighed. "When you were a baby, you started to run into the road. I spanked you good. I made you cry, but I taught you something about a dangerous thing. Do you understand? I was acting for your own good."

Shut up, Finn thought, just shut up and don't ever talk to me again.

"Was I wrong?" her mother persisted. "Or did I save you from a terrible accident?"

"This is different," Finn exploded. "This is so different, how can you even make the comparison? It's a stupid example! I'm not a baby! I'm not running into the road. I know how to take care of myself." When her mother stopped for a red light, she jumped out of the car.

She didn't feel like going to school. It was Friday.

What was she going to tell Seth? She dreaded facing him. She'd call him at work, tell him. She went to school, but she might as well not have. At lunchtime she was on her way to the office to use the phone when she ran into Vida.

"Are you sick?" Vida said. "You look awful."

Finn leaned against the wall and blurted out everything.

"How come you didn't tell me?" Vida said.

Finn shook her head. "I don't know, Vida. You've been pushing Jerry at me . . ."

"You shouldn't have told your mother anything," Vida said. "Why didn't you use your head, say you were going to the movies with me?"

"I don't know," Finn said in a depressed voice. "I didn't think of it."

Vida gave her a look as if she were a child who hadn't yet figured out the big, grown-up world. "You shouldn't be getting all messed up over this guy, anyway, Finn. First he's too old for you—"

"Vida, don't you start!"

"—and second, Jerry is—oh, speak of the devil."

Jerry was approaching. "Hi, girls." His heavy-lidded gaze drifted over her. Finn's face heated, her stomach lurched. Sex, sex. Why did Jerry have this power over her, even at a moment when she felt so awful?

He squeezed her shoulder. "What are you two up to?"

Vida tossed her head flirtatiously. "You know us, Jerry, innocent as two babies."

"Oh, Vida, I know how innocent you are."

"Naughty!"

Finn only half listened to the banter. Time was passing. She had to get in touch with Seth. She started off, leaving Jerry and Vida together. "Have to make a phone call," she said, over her shoulder. Vida would reproach her later for being rude to Jerry. But it was Seth she was thinking of, not Jerry. Then the bell rang, and she drifted off to her next class. Anyway, phoning was so cowardly. As soon as she put it to herself that way, she knew she had to tell Seth to his face.

She skipped out on last period and took the bus downtown. The bus was nearly empty, except for an old woman with knees curved outward like broken sticks. Sad. Finn felt unbearably depressed.

Downtown she walked slowly to the Apple Cafeteria. Inside a wave of hot, smoky air poured over her. Worn plastic banquettes lined the sides of the room. At the counter a line of people moved slowly along, putting dishes on green plastic trays.

An older man with a Hitler mustache was behind the counter. A plastic badge on his jacket said MANAGER. Seth came out of the kitchen and got behind the counter. He was wearing the same red jacket and the same little red bow tie as the manager.

Finn took a tray. "Help you, miss?" Seth winked at her, almost imperceptibly gesturing toward the manager.

"Coke," she said.

"Large?"

She shook her head.

"Medium? Small?" His eyes were warm.

"Medium, please." *Seth I can't go out with you.* She rehearsed the words. Seth scooped crushed ice into a glass, held it under a spigot, then brought it to her on a little saucer and handed her a straw and a napkin.

"Anything else?"

She shook her head. She paid and took her Coke to a table and sat down. She drank the Coke slowly. The line at the counter shortened. The manager went into the kitchen, and Finn got in line again.

"Hey, how are you?" Seth said this time.

"Okay. Seth—I—" but his boss reappeared. Finn sat down again. She chewed on the ice in the glass. When the ice was gone, she rolled the straw up into a thick wad, then unrolled it.

Seth began clearing tables, working his way toward her. He stacked cups and saucers on a rolling cart, wiped out ashtrays, wiped the tables with a wet rag. He came nearer and nearer to her table. Then he was there. "Finished, miss?" His eyes were laughing.

"Seth, I can't go out with you tonight." Oh, God. The words had come out flat and ordinary, as if she didn't care.

He put her empty Coke glass on the rolling cart. "Why?"

"My mother won't let me." She watched as he wiped the table. Big knuckles, healthy-looking nails.

"Why?" he said again.

She licked her lips. "Two reasons. Because you're Jim's brother, and—"

"Jim's a very dangerous character."

"—your age," she said flatly.

"My age? What about my age?"

"She says you're too old for me."

"I don't get it. How old are you?"

"Fifteen."

"Fifteen?" She nodded. "You're fifteen?" he repeated. "I didn't know that."

"Well, didn't Maggie say—"

"No. She didn't say anything about your age. And I just assumed—"

"You thought I was older?"

"Sure, of course I did. I thought you were sixteen, anyway, maybe seventeen? How the hell did I know? I didn't think about your age. You don't look fifteen. I just figured—"

"I'm fifteen," she said again.

"Fifteen," he said. He had stopped wiping the table. He was running his hand through his hair in a distracted way.

Finn stood up. "I don't see what my age has to do with anything," she said.

"No, it's just—"

The manager was looking their way. She zipped up her jacket. She could feel the whole day caving in on her. "Well. You don't want to lose your job. I'd better go." She felt a flicker of pride that she was so calm when she felt so terrible, so really awful. "I'll see you around," she said. And she walked out, crossed the street, and didn't look back. She just kept walking till she got to the bus stop.

10

Standing in front of the mirror over her bureau, Finn stuck out her tongue, then put her hands to her neck, feeling for swollen glands. Her mother stopped at her door. "Aren't you going to school?"

Finn blew her nose on a sock. "I'm sick."

"You look okay to me."

"Some nurse."

"Does anything hurt?" her mother said crisply.

"Everything." She fell back on the bed and pulled the blanket over her head.

Friday, coming home from seeing Seth, she had still been wrapped up in her pride. But once safely in the house, her pride, or her dignity, or whatever it was that had kept her together, began to shred. Vida had called on Saturday to see how the thing with Seth had gone. "I don't want to talk about it," Finn had said and hung up.

All weekend she had felt worse and worse. Now it was Monday, and she felt so bad, she didn't see how she was going to keep on going. She knew what it was—heartsick. Lovesick. Sick. Sick. Sick. Just plain sick of being fifteen and treated like a cretin.

Not enough that her mother pulled that you're-only-fifteen-and-don't-know-your-own-mind number on her. But Seth! Had she wanted the impossible? For him to think of her as *her*? Not as Finn-who-is-only (gasp)-fifteen? Just as her, Finn, someone he liked.

Her mother brought her a glass of orange juice and two aspirin. "Take this," she said. "Your eyes do look kind of red."

Finn slept all morning and woke up feeling awful. Her head hurt, her eyes ached, her chest was tight and painful. She lay in bed, staring out the window and sighing. Steam hissed in the radiators. At least if Seth had acted upset. But why should he? He probably had a string of girl friends a mile long. One for every day of the week. Finn for Friday, Sally for Saturday, Sara for Sunday, Monica for Monday, Toby for Tuesday—

Toby! Toby, Future Kindergarten Teacher. Toby and Seth. Finn sat up, grinding her teeth jealously, then fell back on her pillow with a loud whimper. "Oh! Oh!" Tears filled her eyes. She had never felt so sorry for herself, so bad.

Suddenly she jumped out of bed, scattering the blankets. She was sick of feeling so self-pitying. What did she care who was Seth's girl friend? Toby, or Tabby, or Tibby, all three of them could have him!

Her room was a mess. She kicked at a pile of clothes

on the floor. She pulled on jeans and a sweater and tied her hair back. In the kitchen she opened the refrigerator, then stood inside the door, wondering if she was hungry. No. She picked up a piece of dry toast from the counter and nibbled it.

Shoving her bare feet into boots she went outside for an icicle. Frozen falls of snow lay on the spruce. The sky was a powdery blue. She cracked a glassy icicle free from the porch roof and went back upstairs, sucking on it.

She wandered dispiritedly into the living room and flipped on the TV. On the screen a couple were caressing a car wrapped in ribbons. Irritated, she turned off the machine.

She went into the bathroom and sat there for a long time, still feeling sorry for herself. When she flushed, the bowl began to fill with water. She jiggled the handle, but the water kept rising, then with a soft whoosh it overflowed.

She lifted the cover of the tank and moved the copper ball around. The water kept spilling over the bowl and onto the floor. She went out, closing the door. Plunger! Where was the plunger? She checked under the sink, then the broom closet, then the back stairs. No plunger.

In the hall a trickle of water seeped under the bathroom room. She ran down the stairs to the landlords' apartment. "Mr. Kember! Mrs. Kember!" She knocked on their door. "Are you home? Our toilet's overflowing." No answer.

Upstairs again, she called the Barnowskis. The phone rang and rang. She hung up and dialed the hospital.

"Mrs. Rousseau, please, she's an Emergency Room nurse."

"Who?" the switchboard voice said.

"Mrs. Rousseau. Shirley Rousseau." Finn glanced over her shoulder at the hall.

"Is she a patient?" Switchboard asked.

"No, a nurse."

"I see. What floor?"

"Emergency Room."

"Oh. Is this an emergency?"

"Yes!"

She hung on the phone, shifting from foot to foot. She waited and waited . . . She could have choked to death on a bone, or bled to death from a punctured artery, or drowned from an overflowing toilet.

Suddenly there was a loud buzzing and someone said, "This is Extension Three-four—" The line went dead.

Finn threw down bath towels on the floor, then went back to the phone and tried the hospital again. "Shirley Rousseau, please," Finn said enunciating carefully. "She's an—"

"Would you repeat that name, please?"

"Shirley Rousseau. R as in Robert—"

"Is this a patient?"

"Oh, no," Finn groaned.

"She is not a patient?" Switchboard said in her best robot manner. "Would you please hold for a moment?" The line went dead. Or maybe she was on Hold. Whichever. Finn hung up and this time dialed Maggie's. And if Seth happened to answer? "I'll be totally cool," she murmured. Brisk. Matter-of-fact. *Please check if Maggie has a toilet bowl plunger.* A very sophisticated line. The hell with it. Who cared? The hell with him.

"Hello," a male voice said.

Not Seth. "Jim? This is Finn. I'm sick, and the toilet overflowed, and I can't find the plunger, and I've looked everywhere for it. Do you have a plunger?"

"Sure. Want me to airmail it to you?"

"Jim, don't be funny. I didn't know who else to call."

"Today must be your lucky day," he said cheerfully. "I just came in from the library, and Maggie's here, too. Her afternoon off. Want us to come over and help you?"

"*Would* you?" she said gratefully.

"Who else is there?" he said.

"No one. It's all right. Mom's at work."

"Hang on. Be there in a few minutes."

Finn tottered to a chair. Five minutes later Maggie and Jim walked in. "We came bearing gifts," Jim said. He was carrying a looped metal cable over the shoulder of his camel-hair coat, while Maggie wielded a green rubber plunger.

Maggie looked around. "How weird to be in the house again. When's Mom coming home?"

"About an hour," Finn said. "Thanks for coming, I was desperate."

Maggie opened the bathroom door. "What a mess. Finn, you fool, those are Mom's good towels. Get the washer going, let's do them quick before she comes home."

Jim rolled up his pants and took off his shoes and socks. "You look like you're going in for another Polar Bear dip," Maggie said, as he disappeared into the bathroom. She and Finn went into the kitchen and threw the towels into the washer. Maggie made herself a cheese sandwich. "Bite?" she said to Finn.

There was a clanging noise coming from the pipes, as Jim worked the metal snake. "I haven't eaten all day," Finn said. She sighed. "I feel like hell."

"What's wrong?"

"Remember I told you Seth asked me to go to a movie?"

"I remember. How was it? You and Seth get along?"

"We didn't go. Didn't he say anything to you?"

Maggie took the last bite of her sandwich. "No, I don't see that much of him. He's working all the time. We just sort of wave in passing."

"Well, Mom wouldn't let me go with him, because he's Jim's brother, and—"

"That's so narrow-minded!"

"—besides that, she said, *he's* too young, and *I'm* too old—" Finn heard her goof too late. Maggie burst out laughing. "Don't!" she exclaimed. It was as if Maggie were laughing at *her*, not her goof. Finn, you fool, she'd said. That's what Finn felt like. A fifteen-year-old fool.

Just then they heard the front door open. "Finn?" her mother called. Maggie covered her mouth. "Whose car is in the driveway?" Her mother came down the hall, her arms full of grocery bags.

At the same moment Jim emerged from the bathroom. He was still barefoot.

Finn's mother looked at him, then at Maggie. Her face flushed. "Maggie," she said quietly.

"Hello, Mom."

"What are you doing here?"

"Finn called and—"

"The toilet overflowed," Finn said.

Jim rolled down his shirt-sleeves. "It's fine now, Mrs. Rousseau. I took care of it. Here, let me help you with those." He tried to take a grocery bag from her.

"That's all right!" She practically wrestled it back from him and set it on the counter.

"We're just leaving," Maggie said. Her chin went up. "Come on, Jim, put on your shoes!"

"Let me pay you for your time," Finn's mother said, opening her purse.

"Mom!" Maggie's freckles stood out like copper coins.

How could her mother be that way, Finn thought. It was really insulting to offer money. As if Maggie and Jim were strangers who wanted money for helping out. "Why don't you at least give them a cup of tea?" Finn said.

"We don't need anything," Maggie said quickly.

There was a tense moment of silence, then Finn's mother said, "Sit down. Please." She filled the teakettle and put it on the stove. "Everybody, sit down." Maggie and Jim glanced at each other, then Maggie shrugged and pulled out a chair.

Finn's mother opened a box of crackers and put cream cheese on a plate. "Sit down—Jim," she said. They all sat down around the table.

Finn was amazed. She never thought her mother would do it. . . . What a difference from the last time Maggie and Jim were here and announced they were moving in together! Mostly what she remembered from that night was everyone shouting at everyone else, and

Maggie going back and forth to Jim's car with her things.

Her mother had turned so she was looking at Maggie, just eating her up with her eyes. "It's been a long time," she said.

"Almost five months," Maggie agreed.

Finn imagined the headlines. RECONCILIATION OF MOTHER AND DAUGHTER BROUGHT ABOUT BY PLUGGED TOILET. Wonderful. She ought to feel really happy. But all she could think was that her mother had ruined everything for her with Seth, because he was Jim's brother. And now Jim was here in their house, sitting at their table, drinking their tea and eating their crackers and cheese, as if he'd never been anything but welcome.

11

"Look for an act of kindness from someone close," Finn read aloud. "Your love life is due to change for the better." She was sprawled across Vida's bed. It was Tuesday night, and they were supposedly doing homework, but not much work had been done, what with doing horoscopes, talking about Seth, and idly watching a rerun of *Gilligan's Island* on Vida's tiny TV.

"So tell me again," Vida said. "Was Seth mad?"

"No, surprised. He thought I was older."

"How old? That's nice."

"No. it's not nice, Vida. You should have seen his face. As if fifteen is a disease, and it's catching. How can it be *nice* when I'll probably never see him again? Jesus, Vida, I feel so depressed."

"You don't have to feel that way," Vida said. "If you put your mind to it, you could like Jerry as much as Seth." She had on her practical-recipe voice. "He's cute, he's fun, and he's here! A super guy like him isn't going to be up for grabs much longer. I bet he's a fantastic kisser, too."

"Oh, he's good," Finn said as if she'd had dozens of boys to compare him to. "It was interesting—"

"Interesting! Finn, you're supposed to kiss with your lips, not your mind."

"No, I mean it *was* exciting, but I was aware that it was exciting." She lay back thinking that if Seth had kissed her it would be different. The whole world would disappear. She'd be out of it. Gone. Good-bye! Just thinking about it, she got these electric jolts in her belly.

Vida jiggled Finn's foot. "Wake up. I have an idea. Fleetwood Forest is going to be at the War Memorial Friday. Paul and I have tickets. Why don't you and Jerry come, too?"

"Just like that?" Finn said. "I didn't hear Jerry saying anything."

Vida picked up the phone on her night table. "I'll fix that. I'll call Jerry right now. I know we can get tickets."

"Vida, I don't know—" Finn sighed. "I don't feel about Jerry the way I do about Seth."

"Why not?" Vida's horn-rimmed glasses gave her a stern look. "I mean, what's missing? I don't think you've really tried with Jerry."

Finn shook her head. Vida was right in a way. She ought to just forget Seth. Put him out of her mind. Don't ever say his name again. It hurt to talk about him, and yet she went on doing it.

Vida was dialing. Then asking for Jerry. She held her hand over the phone and said, "You're going to be awfully glad about th—oh, Jerry? Hi. This is Vida. Hi yourself, good-looking."

She bantered with him for a few minutes, then told him about the concert. "I thought you and Paul and Finn and I could all go together—oh. Oh, darn, I forgot! Finn's going to be so disappointed. She's right here." She held out the phone.

"Hello, Jerry," Finn said, shaking her fist at Vida.

"Hi, there. How're you? Looks like we're going to miss. I've got a game Friday night in Cortland."

"I'm sorry," Finn said.

YOU DON'T SOUND SORRY, Vida scrawled on a piece of paper, holding it up in front of Finn. TRY HARDER.

"I've been thinking about you, babes," Jerry said. "Guess where I am right now? Lying here on my bed." He dropped his voice. "Wish you were here."

Finn laughed. She really wasn't good at this sex talk. She'd only managed on New Year's Eve because she'd been swilling down the punch.

"I'm super-sorry about the concert," he said. "We'll try again, babes."

"Okay," she said. "Great." She felt like a hypocrite. When she hung up, she said to Vida, "It didn't work. Negative, Vida."

"You can be so stubborn," Vida said. "You want to come to the concert with me and Paul, anyway? It'll cheer you up."

Finn nodded. "Thanks, Vida," she said. It was horrible feeling the way she did. Empty inside, cheated. It was as if she'd been holding an armful of silver- and gold-wrapped presents, and then, for no reason, someone had knocked them out of her arms. Out of sight, out of reach. Gone forever. Her mother had done that to her.

But as she thought it, Finn wondered if she'd been just too quick to do exactly what her mother told her. Finn had raged and screamed, but she should have thought for herself. Gone downtown to the Apple, all right! But instead of bleating, "I'm fifteen," she should have told Seth not to pick her up at home, but to meet her at the theater.

She sat up. Who would have known the difference? What was it Vida had said? *You don't have to tell your parents everything.* But it was too late now. She'd done it. Good obedient little automaton. She'd done it!

Friday it was snowing again, big fat white flakes coming down thick and fast. Finn wore her long green coat. The bus they took downtown was warm, wet, and steamy. Paul was wearing a peaked ski cap set back on top of his big curly head. "You look cute, Paul," Finn said.

A couple of girls in tight jeans and western jackets were looking at Paul. "Don't I know you?" he said. "From my father's store, I think. Valdone's, in the Mall."

"Right! You sold us the cheese with the black spots."

Vida poked Finn. "Every time we go out, he's coming on with the girls. You should have seen him with Brenda Beech yesterday afternoon."

"I did," Finn said. Paul had had his arm around Brenda, who looked impressive in a flaming red dress.

"I was just telling her she had the best voice in chorus," Paul said.

"I'd have a good voice, too, if I weighed two hundred pounds," Vida said.

"Come on, Vida," Paul said, "let it go."

A freezing blast of wind hit them as they got off the bus. Snow seemed to be pouring out of the sky. Cars could barely move. All the entrances to the War Memorial were jammed with people waiting to get into the concert.

"Fleetwood Forest isn't here yet," someone in line ahead of them said. "I heard their plane is late."

Inside people were wandering around everywhere. They found seats. It was chilly in the big, concrete-floored auditorium. "You know when it's going to start?" A girl sitting in front of them twisted around. She had bangs down to her eyes. "I came early to get a good seat, and now they're late. Isn't that a bummer?"

Across the room Paul saw a boy he knew. "It's Dave Stark," he said. "Let's go talk to him, Vida."

"Want to come, Finn?" Vida said.

"Go ahead. I'll wait here." She didn't want to be a third wheel. Stamping her feet to keep them warm, she looked around. The War Memorial could hold thousands of people. She tried to guess how many there were. Two thousand? Three thousand? She wasn't sure. Most of them were kids. The storm must have kept a lot of people away.

More than an hour passed. Paul and Vida still hadn't returned. She stood up, looking around for them. A man was calling for attention over the PA system. "I have an announcement to make. Quiet, please!" He was wearing a dark jacket and held on to the microphone with both hands. "Because of the storm, our stars, Fleetwood Forest, I regret to say . . . I must tell you, have regrettably been unable to get through to Syr—"

A stream of groans, boos, and hisses drowned the rest of his statement. People began streaming toward the exits.

"Please," the man said, "one more announcement. The State Police have informed me that all major roads out of Syracuse are closed. Those of you who have come here from elsewhere may have to spend the night here. All of Central New York is being covered by a major blizzard. In Syracuse the buses are having problems. Those of you who do not have any place to go can spend the night—"

Finn pulled on her coat. Mobs of people milled around. She got up on a chair to see if she could spot Paul and Vida.

Someone tugged at her coat.

She looked down. It was Seth. "What a place to meet." Holding his sheepskin jacket over his shoulder, he smiled at her.

Her neck turned rigid. She stared at him. "I'm looking for friends," she said at last.

"Maybe they're waiting for you at the entrance."

"Maybe." She jumped down off the chair. Now that she was looking at him—the real Seth, not the one in her imagination—nothing was happening the way she'd thought. In fact the very opposite. Instead of being overcome with joy, she was starting to boil inside.

She started moving toward the entrance, following the crowd. Seth was next to her. She held her head high and said nothing. If the crowd hadn't been so dense, she would have walked away from him as fast as her legs would carry her.

"I didn't know you were coming to the concert," he said.

She gave him a swift look. "Why should you?"

"Oh, it's just that Maggie didn't mention it."

"Maggie doesn't know my business."

A couple of tall, skinny boys elbowed past. "Be careful!" Seth grabbed Finn's arm to steady her.

Finn shook free. Her heart was pounding rapidly. He was trying to charm her! It was outrageous. It made her furious.

"How are you getting home?" he said.

"I'll manage." She kept looking around for Paul and Vida. She'd already decided to call her mother.

"I have a feeling you're mad at me," he said.

"*What?*" She stopped dead. People streamed around them. "Mad at you? Why should I be mad at you," she said. "Who are you that I should be mad at you?"

A painful smile crossed his face. "You *are* mad at me," he said. "I wish you weren't."

"What difference does it make?" she demanded. Her cheeks blazed. "Don't bother yourself. Look, I'm fifteen. Remember? So it doesn't make any difference what I feel, okay?"

She started to move ahead. He caught her arm. "Finn, listen—"

"Listen to what? And let go of me! I can stand on my own two feet."

People glanced at them. She didn't care! Let them hear! Great! Let the whole city hear!

"Would you just tell me why you're so mad?" he said.

"I'd be glad to," she said with icy courtesy. "If you remember the day I came down to the Apple—"

"I remember."

"—and told you what my mother said—" Oh, damn! Her voice was starting to betray her. Shaking. He nodded, waiting for her to go on. They were the same height, and he was looking straight into her eyes. "—and what *you* said," she went on rapidly, "then you should know why I'm mad."

"What'd I say?" He shook his head. "I don't remember saying anything."

"Oh, come on!" she cried. "Don't cop out on me like that."

"No, I mean it. Did I say something to offend you?"

"Oh, no," she said. "Oh, no, you just implied my mother was right, and fifteen was too young for us to be friends." She pulled away from him and moved toward the line of people waiting to use the phones. He stuck with her. She got in line and he stood next to her.

"Finn, listen, if I really said that—I don't think I said that—"

"I don't remember your exact words," she said coolly, "but you can take my word for it, that's what you implied. It definitely was."

"It was an assy thing to say. Or imply."

She stared at him.

"I apologize," he said.

She didn't know how to take this. What were his motives? Did he mean it? Why should he apologize to her? Maybe he was afraid Maggie would get mad at him and kick him out.

A woman in a purple pantsuit walked up and down the line urging people to keep their calls short. "Please consider others," she yelled, making a megaphone of her hands.

"Finn, do you accept my apology?" Seth said. "I'm really sorry. I guess I was pretty surprised when you told me how old you were."

"How young, you mean," she said, not ready yet to relent.

"I'm glad I ran into you tonight," he said, "so we could get this straightened out. I was thinking maybe I'd see you at your sister's sometime."

She shook her head. "I don't see Maggie that much. She's pretty busy."

"Now she's got me there, too," Seth said. "I don't know how long I'll stay there, though. It's awfully close quarters with my brother."

It was Finn's turn at a phone. Her mother picked it up on the second ring. "I'm still in the War Memorial," Finn said.

"There's an incredible blizzard out there," her mother said.

"I know, that's what they told us. They said the buses are breaking down."

"I think I'll drive down and get you," her mother said. "Otherwise no knowing when you'll get home. Wait for me at the Montgomery Avenue entrance. It'll probably take me half an hour. At least," she added.

"She's coming for you?" Seth said after Finn hung up. "Think she'll have any trouble?"

"She'll make it," Finn said. "She's a good driver. A little snow won't stop her."

"That's confidence."

"Don't forget she's the wife and I'm the daughter of a long-distance hauler."

Seth smiled. "I'll wait with you, if that's okay."

"It's okay." She looked around. "Except I should find my friends."

"Do you think they left?" She shook her head. "Maybe we should wait in one place," he said. "Not go round in circles."

They found a spot near the ticket window. The doors kept opening and closing. The floor was a slushy mess. Outside the snow was falling, falling, falling.

"Do you fight a lot in your family?" Seth said.

Finn stared at him, "No. Why?"

He laughed. "That came out wrong. I didn't mean to insult you. It's just—you're such a fierce fighter. You were the same way at your sister's—remember? When you got mad at her—fierce!" He sounded admiring. "Are you always like that?"

"Oh, no!" Finn didn't want him to think she was quarrelsome. "I just get so teed off sometimes, I say whatever comes into my head. Was I awful just now?"

"You were great! No, I mean it. There are some people who are cool about everything. My father is more or less like that. That's why we don't get along. No matter how mad he gets at me, he won't fight."

"What does he do?"

Seth smiled wryly. "Depends. Slams doors. Calls a few names. Walks out. Stuff like that. It's refreshing to meet someone who knows how to fight. I admit it was a little tough being on the receiving end, but in a way I liked it."

"Oh, now I understand," she said. "You're a masochist. I'll have to remember to get mad at you regularly."

"That's right," he said. "Keep me in line."

It didn't pass Finn by that they were speaking as if they were going to see each other again.

"Finn!" She turned, hearing her name. It was Vida and Paul. "There you are," Vida said. "Where have you been? We looked everywhere for you."

"Vida, Paul, this is Seth," Finn said. Vida's eyes got big. Paul and Seth shook hands. "Mom's coming down for me," Finn said, "so hang around and she'll drive you home."

Vida tugged at Paul's arm. "Listen, Finn, we'll be over there." She pointed across to the other side of the entrance hall. "Just yell for us."

"You can stay here," Finn said, but Vida was already dragging Paul off.

"Want to see what it's like out there?" Seth said.

"Sure." She buttoned up her coat and pulled on her hat. Outside the wind was howling, but beneath the shelter of the overhang it was relatively calm. The streetlights at the corner threw little sprays of pale light on the swirling snow.

"I like winter," Finn said. "I like this crazy weather."

"I know what you mean," Seth said. "It's fierce, but beautiful." He took out a cigarette, then paused. "You mind? You're not a smoker, are you?"

Finn shook her head, and Seth stuck the cigarette

back in his pocket. "Oh, please, if you want to," she said.

"No, that's okay. I don't smoke that much anyway. I can take it or leave it."

"Are you sure?"

"I'm sure." He was half turned toward her, looking at her, a warm look, a warm smile. She had only time to think, He's going to kiss me, when it happened. He put his hands on her shoulders, their lips met, and they were kissing. Her heart took a frightened, ecstatic leap. Seth gripped her arms. She leaned wonderingly into the kiss. His lips were soft.

The lights of an approaching car bounced through the falling snow. They drew apart quickly. The car pulled up to the curb, the horn beeped. "It's my mother," Finn said. She walked toward the car.

"I'll call you," Seth said.

Finn opened the car door. "I have to get Vida and Paul."

"Who was that?" Her mother peered through the curtain of falling snow. Seth was walking down the street. Then Vida and Paul came out of the building, and Finn got into the car next to her mother.

"Mrs. Rousseau," Vida said, "you're an angel! Did you ever meet my boyfriend, Paul Valdone? Was the driving terrible?"

Finn sank back in the seat. She looked out the window. Seth had disappeared. Had it really happened? What did it mean? Again her heart gave that ecstatic, frightened quiver. She leaned her forehead against the cold window. I'm in love, she thought.

12

"Well, what's been happening while I've been gone?" Finn's father pushed up the sleeves of his sweat shirt. He'd been gone over two weeks this time. It was Sunday morning. He had driven most of the night to get home. The big TV was on, and the Sunday paper was scattered over the floor. Her mother, still in her nightgown, had brought in fruit, cocoa, and toast on trays.

"The weather's been miserable," her mother said, taking a bite of toast. "The whole city was closed down Friday night and yesterday. That's our big news."

"Don't tell me," her father said. "I drove blind for the last hundred miles." He put down his cocoa cup.

"What have you been doing, Finn?"

"Not much. I went to a concert Friday, but the group never showed up."

Finn's mother looked at her. "Who was that boy you were talking to when I drove up?"

"Nobody," Finn said. She started peeling a tangerine.

"That's funny. I thought I saw him kissing you."

Finn's face flamed. She tore apart the tangerine and stuck a section in her mouth. Both her parents were watching her. Waiting for her to say something. It made her furious. What business of theirs was it if she kissed someone? She peeled the little strings from another section of tangerine. She knew that wasn't what was really making her mad. It was that she couldn't lead her own life. Couldn't tell them the truth. *I was kissing Seth.* She couldn't even think that and look them in the eyes without being afraid of giving herself away.

"You know I have a funny feeling, I have a hunch," her mother said. There was an old little half-smile on her face. "Stop me if I'm wrong, but I think that boy was the one we were talking about."

"Who's that, Shirl?" Her father turned a page of the newspaper.

"Jim Warenecke's brother," her mother said. "I told you about him asking Finn out, Ted."

Her father's broad face darkened. "I don't want you to have anything to do with that boy, Finn."

"I know, I know. Mom told me all that. And I think you're both wrong." She got a little weak in the knees when she argued with her father, but she wasn't going to give in, either.

"Is my hunch right, Finn?" her mother said.

Finn dropped tangerine peel on the floor. "Damn." She bent over to pick it up. When she straightened up, her mother was looking her right in the face. "Yes, it was Seth," she said reluctantly.

"So I *am* right," her mother said. "That's why you suddenly decided to go to the concert!"

"It is not!" Finn said hotly. "I just bumped into him."

"Quite a coincidence. Four thousand people, and you manage to bump into the one person you're not supposed to see."

"That's what happened," Finn said tensely.

"I don't care how it happened," her father said. "That boy is *off limits*!"

For a moment Finn couldn't speak, then she turned to her mother. "You're so worried about Seth because he's Jim's brother. Why don't you tell Dad what happened when the toilet plugged up? Tell him who was right here in our house!"

"Don't worry," her mother said. "I told him."

"Did you tell him Jim was sitting at our table, drinking out of our cups, and eating our food? And the sky didn't fall in!" Her voice had risen. "You talk like Seth is a pervert, because he's Jim's brother. Jim must be a pervert, too, and he was right here in our house!"

"I want you to quiet down!" Her father leaned toward her. "Now you tell me. What's going on with you and that boy?"

"We're friends."

"Friends?" he said. "Since when are boys and girls friends?"

"Dad! Things have changed."

"That's what I'm afraid of," he said. "Kids are too damn friendly these days."

"I can take care of myself. I'm almost sixteen—"

"You're not sixteen for a good while," her mother said.

"What happens when I am?" she said.

"Maybe we'll all be lucky, and you'll have better sense."

Finn's throat filled. They had so little faith. Just worried that she'd do something wrong, and wrong meant sex. That's what they were afraid of. But that wasn't really *any* of their business. She had a mind of her own. The nutty part was she probably mostly agreed with them about sex. At least if sex meant going all the way. Mr. Merton, in their Family Life classes, had said sex wasn't just intercourse, the way most people thought. It was kissing and petting and loving in lots of other ways.

"Why don't you just come right out and say what you really mean?" Finn said. "Jim had sex with Maggie—" She stammered, her face blazed, but she went on. "—and you're afraid I'll have sex with Seth." There! She had said the truth. "Well, you can stop worrying. I'm not going to."

"It's not only up to you," her father said. "There are a lot of things you don't understand yet."

Her mother put down her cup. "He's too old for you, and there are other complications. You know what they are. Don't think, because Maggie was here for one hour, one afternoon, the facts have changed."

"What do I do if he's at Maggie's when I visit?" Finn said. "Does that mean I can't look at him? Or talk to him? Or are you going to forbid me to see my own sister?"

"Yes, I'm going to forbid you if he's there!"

"How will you know?"

"We trust you to do what we say," her father put in.

"Trust me? If you really trusted me, you'd let me go out with him." Infuriatingly her eyes filled with tears.

"It's settled," her father said. "You're not seeing him, Finn."

The phone rang. Finn stood up, thinking it might be Seth.

"I'll take it," her father said, as if he'd read her mind. He went ahead of her down the hall. "Hello? Who?" He looked at Finn. "Who is this? . . . No. No, I'm sorry. No, you can't. We don't want you calling her." He hung up.

"That was Seth," Finn said. Her father nodded. She was stunned. "He called to talk to me. Why didn't you give me the phone?"

"We told you, Finn—"

"I can't believe this," she said. "Why are you doing this to me? Do you hate me?"

"Make an effort and try to understand," her father said. "What your mother and I are doing is for your own good."

Finn walked away without replying. She would never understand—not what they meant by understanding. It was inhuman. They wanted her to turn off her feelings as if she were some sort of faucet. Pretend she'd never met Seth. Don't see him. Don't think about him.

She put on her jacket and hat and went outside. Huge snowbanks towered at every corner. Red flags were stuck in them to warn motorists. She felt like sticking her head into a snowdrift, gulping lumps of ice, letting them slide down her throat into the center of herself.

She threw a snowball. It smashed against a tree, leaving a white spatter. She threw another, another, another, until her arm ached. No. They couldn't stop her. She was going to see Seth. She had to. She packed snow. "I will see him," she said. She threw. "I will. I will. I will."

13

Monday after school Finn stopped in Nick's Pizzeria to use the phone. It was a narrow little place with half a dozen tiny tables, and a phone next to a soft-drink machine. She didn't want to risk calling the Apple from home. Her father was home.

"Apple," a man said. She asked for Seth. "Just a moment." The counterman was watching her.

"Hello?"

"Seth," she said. "It's me, Finn." Her face blazed.

"I called you yesterday," he said.

"I know. My father—I'm sorry."

"Rough," he said.

"Did you want to talk to me about anything special?"

"No, I just thought we'd talk. I'd like to get to-gether—" His voice dropped off. Then he said, "but I don't want to make trouble for you."

"No, don't worry about that," she said. "They don't

want me to see you, but I told them, what if you're at Maggie's when I visit her."

"What'd they say?"

"They didn't know what to say. They can't forbid me to see my own sister. I'm going to be sixteen in May. That's not so far away."

"Do you think you could come down to the Apple? We could talk."

"What about tomorrow after school?" she said. "I think I can do that."

"Sure, that would be great," he said.

"I'll be there." A smile spread uncontrollably across her face.

"I'll be looking for you," he said. "I better hang up now. My boss—"

"Okay, sure," she said, but she didn't say good-bye. She didn't want to hang up.

"See you tomorrow then."

"Yes. Tomorrow." She hung up, then just stood there smiling at the phone.

"Get through okay?" the counterman said. His belly bulged beneath his soiled apron.

Finned turned. "Yes, thanks!"

"Your boyfriend?"

"Well . . . I guess he is," she said. "I hope so!" She laughed. "Are you Nick?"

"Tell you a secret. I'm really William. But 'William's Pizzeria' didn't sound so good. You want something? How about a slice of cheese pizza?"

"Sure." She leaned on the counter as he took a hot pie out of the oven and cut a triangular slice. "That smells wonderful." Happiness made her hungry.

The next day she cut her last class and took the bus downtown. It was gray, nasty. Finn was glad to get into the warmth of the Apple. Seth was behind the counter waiting on a couple of old men. The restaurant seemed to be full of old men sitting over coffee cups, talking, and reading their racing sheets. Besides Seth, she was the only young person in the place.

"You got here," Seth said. He was wearing his red nylon jacket and red bow tie.

"Hot chocolate, please," she said. "My feet are freezing. And one of those corn muffins. Are they good?"

Seth put thumb and forefinger together. "Best thing they make in this joint. Use plenty of butter." He put an extra pat on her plate. She took her tray to a corner table. She was excited, chilled, and nervous all at the same time. Someone might walk in who knew her. But why shouldn't she be here? It was a public place.

When there was a lull at the counter, Seth came around and sat down next to her. "Where's your boss?" Finn said, remembering the man with the Hitler mustache.

"Oh, he's in and out."

"He's a grouch, isn't he?" she said.

"That's his first name. Grouch E. Hagen."

"I could tell just by looking at him," Finn said.

"He wouldn't give you the time of day," Seth agreed. "I try to stay out of his way. Just do my job. What are we talking about Hagen for? You know, I'm real glad to see you."

She thought of their kiss. "I'm glad, too. "She couldn't stop smiling.

Someone was at the counter. Seth went to wait on

him. Then a few more people came in, then a whole crowd, and he was busy for a while. She liked watching him work, the way he smiled, and made little jokes with the customers.

There was a clock over the counter. She could stay until 4:30. She had to be home before her mother.

Seth sat down again. "Do your folks know you're here?"

"No way."

"What happens if they find out?"

"I don't know," Finn said. She looked directly at him. "I wanted to come, so I did."

He nodded. "Sometimes that's the only way to do things." He took a bite of her corn muffin.

"You're right," Finn said. "It's really good. Here, take the rest, I had plenty."

"No, I can get all I want. You eat it. Is your birthday really in May?"

"Yes. How'd you know that?"

He laughed. "You said so on the phone."

"I did? I don't remember."

"My birthday's in May, too. May twentieth."

"Mine's the twenty-fourth." There was that number four again. Four days between their birthdays. "I'm Gemini," she said. "You're Taurus."

"I'll take your word for it."

She made horns at her forehead. "Taurus! Olé!"

"You have nice hands," he said. "I always notice people's hands." He took her hands and held them against his. Their hands were about the same size, but his fingers were thicker.

"Aha, there's your good-luck ring," he said. "Has it brought you any good luck lately?"

"Oh, a little," she said. "I was wearing it Friday night." She had half a dozen little silver-and-turquoise rings on each hand.

"Where'd you get them all?" he said.

"My father brought them to me at different times, from New Mexico, mostly. They're Navajo." She touched a ring with three tiny turquoises. "This is my favorite."

"I like this one," he said, touching a plain silver band.

"You really like that best? Here—it's yours." She took it off. "Give me your hand—"

"No, I can't," he said. "I mean, it's yours."

"I want you to have it," she said. She pushed the ring onto his pinkie. He didn't wear any jewelry.

"Thanks," he said. He looked terribly pleased.

They sat there with their fingers intertwined. She thought she could sit there, just that way, forever, feeling the weight and warmth of his hand on hers.

They started talking about school, and he told her he'd dropped out because he didn't feel he was learning anything. "My best friend moved away that year, too. And I was fighting a lot with my father. I had to get out of the house."

"Where was your mother?"

"She split a long time ago, when I was in junior high."

"Do you see her?"

"I did when I was out in California." There was that same open, painful smile she'd seen on his face at the

War Memorial. It hurt her. She wanted to make him feel better.

"Is your father nice?" she asked.

"I don't know. We don't agree on much of anything. He thinks I'm crazy to want to farm. But he has this fixed idea that Jim's going to be the doctor, like him. And I'll be the lawyer. Never," he said. "Lawyers are bores." They looked at each other and laughed.

"I have to go in a few minutes," she said.

"I want to write down my hours for you. Got a piece of paper?" She tore out a sheet of notepaper and gave it to him. "I wish you didn't have to go," he said. "Are your feet warm now?" He handed her the piece of paper.

She put on her hat. She had her green coat around her shoulders. They looked at each other. Did he want to kiss her? She wanted to kiss him. Just thinking it turned her hot and shivery.

"Button up your coat," he said. "It's cold outside."

She tucked her books under her arm. An old man wearing a blue vest and a ski cap looked at her. No, she couldn't kiss him here. It was too public. Too bad! She glanced at the clock. It was late. "Seth, I have to fly!" She'd already stayed ten minutes longer than she should have.

When she got home, her father was sleeping on the couch. Her mother came in about fifteen minutes later. Finn was in her room doing homework.

"Finn," her mother said, "where were you? I called home to ask you to get supper started. Your father said you hadn't come in yet."

Finn's heart jumped. "I went downtown. Vida

wanted to look for a blouse." The lie came out before she knew she was going to say it. It was that easy.

"Did she get something?"

Finn glanced down at her history book. "No, she couldn't find anything she liked." Didn't her mother know, just by the tone of her voice, that she was lying?

After supper her parents went to a movie, and Finn ran across their yard to the Barnowskis. Vida's little sister, Karen, let her in. "Vida's in her room, Finn." Karen was wearing blue Dr. Denton's. "Vii-daaa," she yelled, "here comes Finn to see youuuu."

Mrs. Barnowski called hello from the living room, and Mr. Barnowski said, "Cold enough for you, Finn?"

She went up the stairs to Vida's room. Vida was brushing her hair.

"Vida, hi. I need your help." Finn sat down on the edge of the bed. "My mother thinks I was with you after school."

Vida looked at her through a curtain of hair. "Where were you?"

"In the Apple with Seth."

"You're kidding."

"No, really. I cut seventh period."

"I thought your parents told you he was a no-no."

"Vida!" Finn slapped her hand against the wall, hitting one of Vida's travel posters. "You're the one who always says they don't have to know everything."

"I'm just trying to get things straight," Vida said calmly. "When you told me about the fight you had with your parents . . . I don't know, but somehow, I wasn't exactly sure what you were going to do."

"I told you! I'm sure I told you. I said they weren't going to stop me."

Vida shrugged. "Okay, so now I know. What'd you tell them about today?"

"I said I was with you, shopping."

"No problem. But next time, definitely warn me in advance."

"It's so upsetting!" Finn exclaimed. She'd always thought being in love would be wonderful and simple. "I don't like lying to my mother."

"Who does?" Vida went on vigorously brushing her hair, and counting under her breath.

"I just never thought everything would be so complicated," Finn said.

Vida straightened up. "Let me tell you something, Finn. If you want things to be nice and simple, do what your parents want. Right? Forget about Seth."

Finn shook her head. "No, Vida!" Just thinking that her parents could dictate to her that way turned her hot with fury and frustration. "No," she said again. "No!" She welcomed the anger. It was clean and simple, and helped wipe out the bad feeling she had from lying. She wasn't just being defiant. It was much more than that, so much more than asserting herself. It was Seth. Yes, that's what it was really about. Seth. Seth and Finn. Finn and Seth.

14

In the next couple of weeks a certain table in the corner at the Apple became Finn's table. Whenever she could get downtown to the Apple, she followed the same routine. She'd buy hot chocolate and a corn muffin, then spread her books at "her" table. Slowly sipping the cocoa, she'd do homework till Seth could join her. The Apple was like a club, always full of the same gray old men with their coffees, their newspapers, and their racing sheets.

There were plenty of free tables. No one bothered Finn, or said anything about her taking up a table for an hour or more. Seth worked hard, waiting on customers, cleaning tables, sweeping the floor, but there were always moments when he had nothing to do and could take a break.

Then, their heads close together, they'd hold hands, talking and even kissing. It was like a dream. Finn would forget that other people were nearby. It was as if they were alone, just the two of them in their own little corner of the world.

Sometimes on her lunch hour, Finn went out of school and called Seth from Nick's Pizzeria. If Seth's boss, Mr. Hagen, answered, he always said Seth was busy and hung up on her. Sometimes Seth called her at home after school, before her mother was back from work. Her father was out on the road again. Once or twice Seth had to hang up fast when her mother came home early. But their conversations were always brief, anyway, because Seth was calling from the Apple.

Friday night at the movies was the one place they could meet without worrying. Vida helped her. It was a lot better than the Apple. One Friday Mrs. Barnowski drove the two girls downtown. She was going to play bingo after she dropped them.

"Your mother say anything?" Vida said in a low voice.

Finn glanced at Mrs. Barnowski in the front seat. "No." Without realizing it, Finn had always assumed her parents could see through her and into her. Transparent Finn. They were supposed to know when she was deceiving them. But, clearly, they didn't.

"Sometimes I wish they would say something, Vida," she said. "I really hate lying to them. It's so ugly." She didn't actually think about it when she was with Seth, but at home her stomach was always in a knot.

"Don't be an idiot," Vida said. "If it was up to them, you wouldn't ever see Seth."

"I know," Finn said.

Vida squeezed Finn's hand. Now that Finn was in

love, they were closer than ever. "I remember how crazy I used to be about Paul . . ." Vida leaned back so her mouth was close to Finn's ear. "I could hardly eat. It was just . . . Paul, Paul, Paul." Vida shook her head. "Now sometimes he can make me climb walls. He has these things he says . . . little phrases . . . he's always repeating them. Like, 'sol-id!' " She imitated Paul's voice. "Sometimes I think if he says that just one more time—"

Mrs. Barnowski pulled up in front of the movie theater. "Here we are, girls. See you at ten thirty, right?"

The girls got out. "Thanks, Mrs. B.," Finn said. It was still early. They bought their tickets and went inside to wait in the lobby.

"The other day we had Paul's whole house to ourselves," Vida said. Finn looked at her curiously. Vida nodded. "We did it. I didn't feel like it, but Paul did. After, Finn, I felt so depressed, and Paul didn't even know it. That made it even worse."

"Why'd you do it if you didn't want to?"

"You don't know, do you?" Vida said. "You'll find out. You can't just say yes one day, and no thank you the next."

"Well, I'm sure no one feels the same way every time," Finn said.

"That's true. It's hard to explain, Finn, it's just not simple. Oh, look—" She pinched Finn's arms. "There's Seth. God, he's gorgeous."

In a few minutes Paul also appeared, and they went into the movie house. Paul and Vida sat way in back. Finn and Seth found seats close to the front. They sat next to each other, holding hands, their heads touching.

The theater was dark. On the screen people were talking. The scene changed. A dog was racing down the road. She hardly paid attention. Seth slipped his arm around her shoulder, his hand dropped lightly onto her breast, their legs were touching. Finn sat quietly, experiencing the most exquisite sensations—it was as if the warmth of the sun was spreading through her, starting in her belly and moving out over her whole body, spreading like liquid through her arms and legs, into her toes and the tips of her fingers. She leaned closer to Seth and put her hand on his thigh.

"I love you," she whispered. She didn't think he heard. But he whispered back. "I love you." Again that radiant sense of warmth went through her. He turned his head. His lips tasted salty, like potato chips.

They met a few Friday nights this way. Then Seth's boss changed his night off, saying Friday was too busy, and he needed Seth. Finn couldn't get out of the house weeknights. They were back to seeing each other a few hours now and then in the Apple.

It was mid-February. The weather stayed clear and icy. The sun shone day after day. But everything seemed to conspire against Finn's and Seth's seeing each other. Her mother came down with a flu and was laid up for a week. Finn went straight home from school to help out. Even after her mother went back to work, she felt tired and was coming home early, some days even before Finn was home from school. Finn didn't dare risk going downtown.

One day, at home, she called Seth at the Apple. "I've missed you," he said.

"I know! Me, too. It's my mother. . . . "

"When do you think you can come down?"

"I don't know." She glanced at the clock. "I'm lucky I could even call you." The doorbell rang. "Ugh! Someone's at the door, I have to hang up."

"Okay, honey. Good-bye."

"Bye," she said reluctantly. The doorbell rang again. "Coming! I'm coming," she yelled.

To her surprise it was Jerry Demas. "Hello, stranger," he said.

"Hi, Jerry." Finn felt awkward. She'd been avoiding him.

"Going to invite me in?" He followed her into the living room and looked around, his thumbs hooked through his belt loops. "Where's your room?"

"What? Down there," she said pointing automatically.

"I'd like to see it." He put an arm around her waist and started walking her down the hall.

"Jerry," she protested. She pulled back, but he was strong—it surprised her how strong he was—and he moved her along easily. "I don't even know if my bed's made," she said, which, under the circumstances, struck her as a truly dumb remark.

In her room Jerry went around looking at everything, at her desk, her books, the pots and tubes of cosmetics on her bureau, her rings on a little metal tree. He actually opened her closet and looked in at her shoes and jeans and shirts.

"*What* are you doing?" she exclaimed.

"Just trying to figure you out."

"Oh, now I get it. Sherlock Demas."

"*Very* funny." He went to the window and looked out. "Nice view."

"Yes, lovely," she said. "You can see every roof in the neighborhood."

He sat down on the bed. "Come here." He grabbed her hand.

"What do you want, Jerry?" She resisted being pulled down next to him. "Let's go in the other room—"

"Wait a minute," he said. "We're going to the hockey game Saturday night."

She stared at him, then shook her head. She yanked her hand free and sat down at her desk. Jerry followed her and sat on the edge of the desk.

"Why not?" he said.

She got herself together. "Jerry, I'm going with someone."

"To the hockey game?"

"No, I mean all the time."

"Who?" he said.

"You don't know him."

"What's his name?"

"It doesn't matter, Jerry."

"Hey, don't give me that. Is it that older guy?"

"Jerry. It doesn't make any difference. What do you want from me?"

"If you don't know by now!"

"Jerry, come on," she said. "Let's be friends."

"I'm for that." Leaning down he put his hands around her face, forcing her mouth to his. She broke free.

"Stop! What are you doing?"

"Kissing you."

"That was more like a slap than a kiss," she exclaimed.

"There are some girls who appreciate the way I kiss," he said, staring at her breasts.

Finn jumped up and walked out of the room. Jerry followed. "Listen," Finn said, "there are lots of girls who'd fall over, if you just looked at them. Why don't you go bother them?"

"You have big problems, Finn," he said going to the door. "When you come right down to it, you're kind of a cold fish." He went down the stairs.

Finn ran out on the landing. "I am, am I?" she yelled. "I know somebody who doesn't think so." But Jerry was already gone.

The next day when she called Seth at the Apple, Mr. Hagen answered. "He's busy!" he barked.

"Well, could you—" she began, but he hung up on her.

After supper her mother was dozing on the couch with the TV turned on low. Finn prowled restlessly around. It had been nearly two weeks since she'd seen Seth. "I miss you," she said under her breath. "I *miss* you!" Saying it made her miss Seth even more. She passed the living room. Her mother sighed in her sleep and turned over. She had an afghan over her shoulders.

"Mom?" Finn whispered. No answer.

She went down the hall to the kitchen, trying to decide if it was safe to call Seth. If her mother woke up, she'd just hang up fast. She dialed the Apple, all the time listening for her mother.

"Apple." She recognized Mr. Hagen's voice and tried to disguise her own. "Seth Warenecke, please."

"Not in!" He hung up.

"Hitler," she exclaimed. She got an apple from the fridge. Was Hagen lying to her? Or was Seth really not working? Maybe he was home, at Maggie's.

She checked her mother again. Still sleeping. She dialed Maggie's number. Maggie answered on the first ring. "Hello, Finn, how's it going?" They talked for a few minutes. Maggie was excited because she'd left her hamburger job. "Good-bye, grease!" she said. She'd found a job as a clerk in a law office.

"Maybe when I go back to school, I'll go for pre-law. It's really interesting."

"Great," Finn said. She remembered how Seth had said lawyers were boring. It made her smile. "I want to speak to Seth," she said, keeping her voice down. She wondered if Maggie could tell, just by the way she said his name, how she felt about him.

"He's not in," Maggie said. "What do you want with Seth, anyway?"

"I want to talk to him." Finn was taken aback by Maggie's abrupt tone, but she laughed and said, "Do I need clearance?"

"Have you two been seeing each other?" Maggie said.

"What?" Finn couldn't believe this. Her sister was giving her the third degree.

"I *said*, Have you two been seeing each other?"

"Not officially," Finn said.

"Finn, I know you're not supposed to see Seth,"

Maggie said evenly. "Officially, or *un*officially. I talked to Mom a couple weeks ago, and I happen to know she was pretty upset about you and Seth at that concert."

"I'm feeling pretty upset myself, right now," Finn said. "What's going on, Maggie? Since when do you agree with Mom and Dad about Seth?"

"Well, Mom and I talked it over. She thinks he's too old for you, and I can see her point."

"Their basic reason for me not to see him is that he's Jim's *brother*," she said heatedly. "Remember? Guilt by association."

"No, you're wrong, it's not that. When you're fifteen, you can be pushed into doing things—"

"Sex," Finn said. Everyone talked about it, as if there were nothing else. "Nobody's pushing me into anything, Maggie. It's the other way around. Mom and Dad are pushing me *away*, trying to keep me from seeing people I want to see—"

"Not people," Maggie corrected. "Just one person. Seth."

"You're really on their side now," Finn said. "What's happened to you, Maggie?"

"Nothing, Finn."

"Yes, it has. You've changed!"

"Look, Finn, the day we were over for the plumbing, we broke the ice with Mom. Mom and I've talked on the phone a few times since then. No big deal, but the way I look at it, it's a beginning. We still have a long way to go. I want to see me and Jim sitting down at the table with Mom and Dad and you like a family, and all the junk we went through forgotten," Maggie said with emotion.

"I want that, too," Finn said. "But I don't see what that's got to do with scuttling me!"

"Don't dramatize yourself," Maggie said sharply. "Let's face it, Finn, you're talking about something that's basically unimportant. A crush. You'll get over it."

"Unimportant," Finn repeated.

"I'm talking about my *life*," Maggie went on. "I'll spell it out for you. I've thought it over, and I'm not going to help you, in any way, break the rules Mom and Dad set down. I happen to think that they're more right than wrong. My advice to you is to cool it. Just do what Mom and Dad say."

"Yes, the way you did," Finn said, so devastated by Maggie's attitude that she could barely speak.

"It's not the same," Maggie said. "And you know it!"

In the living room, her mother stirred. "Finn, are you on the phone?"

"Yes." Finn held the phone away from her ear. Maggie was still talking, but Finn wasn't listening.

15

A few days after her conversation with Maggie, Finn
went down to the Apple after school. Mr. Hagen was
standing behind the counter with Seth, waiting on
people. Finn got a tray. "What can I do for you?" Mr.
Hagen snapped out the words. Finn thought he recognized her. With his little stiff mustache and hair falling
over one eye he looked even more like Hitler. She ordered, and he turned to fix the cocoa.

"Hi," she started to say to Seth. He put his finger to
his lips with a glance at Mr. Hagen.

Finn took her tray and sat down at "her" table. She
opened a book. Mr. Hagen kept looking her way. She
glanced down at the book. She didn't want him to think
she was just hanging out.

About twenty minutes passed. Seth was talking to
Mr. Hagen. Mr. Hagen's face was red. Something was
making him mad. Were they talking about her?

Seth went into the kitchen and a moment later he came out wearing his sheepskin jacket. He didn't look at Finn, but walked by her table and said, "Outside." Then he was past her, zipping up his jacket, pushing through the door. Finn got her stuff together, put on her coat, and buttoned it up. She was aware that Mr. Hagen was watching.

Seth was waiting for her on the corner. He was hatless. The weather was getting warmer. There was a steady drip-drip-drip in the air as snow melted off the roofs. "What's going on?" she said. "What are we doing out here?"

"We're going to spend an hour together like real people," he said, putting his arm across her shoulders.

"What'd you tell your boss?"

"Not half what I wanted to tell him," Seth said. "I just said, Hagen, old chap, I'm taking off."

"Come on, what'd you really say?"

"Told him I was going to leave early."

"What'd he say?"

"He wanted to know why."

"And you said—"

"Well, what I wanted to say was, 'None of your business!' "

"You didn't tell him *that*?" Finn said, laughing.

"No, damn it." Seth looked sheepish. "I didn't know what I was going to say, I just rushed up to him and told him I was going. I said the first thing that came to my mind. I told him I had a toothache."

"A toothache! Good one, good one," Finn said. "Did he believe you?"

"I don't know. Maybe. Did I look like I was in pain?"

"No, but he did!"

"He couldn't say anything anyway," Seth said, "because I've been busting my ass for him for weeks."

"Maybe you shouldn't have done this, though," Finn said. "You know, it's your job."

"Are you kidding? It's the first of March."

"What's that mean?"

"It means that I declare today a holiday. I'm sick of working, and I want to spend time with my girl," he said, looking at her.

She put her arm through his and linked their hands. They wandered around downtown, bumping into each other, going in and out of stores, the library, and then the art museum, looking for somewhere to be alone. Then they walked into the Historical Society Museum, a dark-red brick building that was empty except for a needle-thin woman sitting at the desk downstairs.

Upstairs there was a bench in one of the display rooms. They sat down and began to kiss. Cheeks . . . eyes . . . forehead . . . chin . . . and then mouths. Seth's hands were under Finn's coat. He kissed her breasts through her blouse, then he asked her to take it off.

Dazed and happy, breathing in his smells of wool, skin, and soap, she laughed. "Here?" He nodded. "I can't take off my blouse here," she said.

"Yes, you can. Take it off and keep your coat on."

She looked around. The door was open. There was one window with a venetian blind. "What if someone comes?"

"We'll hear them coming," he said. "The stairs creak."

"It's crazy," she said, sitting up. "I don't want to take off my blouse in a public place."

"I want to look at you," he said.

"Well . . . but . . . *here*?" she said again.

"Where do you suggest?"

"I don't know," she said.

"If it's really going to upset you, forget it."

"You're upset," she said, "not me."

"No, I'm not. Will you pull up your shirt at least?"

"All right." He moved her hand. He was hard under his jeans. She kept thinking someone was coming. It spoiled her pleasure. "Seth, we better stop."

"What's the matter?"

"I'm worried someone will come."

"I told you, there's nothing to worry about."

"That's okay for you to say!"

"Okay, okay." He jumped up and went to the window.

"I don't see why you're mad," she said.

"I'm not mad." He had his back to her.

"You sound it."

"I am not mad!" He snapped up the venetian blind.

She tucked in her blouse. She noticed a rip in the pocket of her coat and absently poked at it. The silence lengthened. He was leaning on his hands, staring out the window. She got up and put her arms around him, her face against his back. "Hello, grumpy. Over here," she said. "Finn," he said, turning around, "this is getting to me. You know what we've been doing? Stealing kisses in the Apple and necking in the Historical Society."

"At least it's educational," she said.

"I just wish we had more time to ourselves. If only we could work something out. If I had a place of my own, a room, we could go there."

"Has it been so terrible?" she said. She had been happy even with just seeing him in the Apple, even with those few kisses, those few precious minutes to talk and be close.

"It hasn't been terrible," he said. "But it's not enough. You know what I mean—I want to sleep with you."

She shook her head. "No, Seth. I'm not going to."

"I knew you'd say that."

"What do you mean?"

"Girls always say no at first."

"I'm not 'girls'! I'm me."

"Don't look so upset," he said.

"I'm not upset." But it hurt her that he seemed so dissatisfied.

They sat down together again and put their arms around each other and kissed. "Finn, I know you haven't done it."

"What's that got to do with it? And how do you know?"

"Didn't you ever hear that boys can tell by the way a girl walks," he teased.

"Baloney!"

"Well, then, by the way you kiss."

"Is there something wrong with the way I kiss? Oh,

you're so *experienced*," she cried, pushing him away. "I suppose you're comparing me to all the other girls you've kissed?"

"You're a wonderful kisser," he said.

"I don't believe you. Tell the truth."

"I love the way you kiss. That's the truth. Now you tell the truth. Are you afraid to make love?"

She shook her head. "No, but I'm not going to. Seth, have you slept with a lot of girls?"

"Enough."

"How many?"

"Nosey."

"Did you love them all?"

"I don't know. Some."

"Some! That sounds like a lot. Was Toby one of them?"

He laughed. "You don't really think I'm going to tell."

She shook his arm. "Tell me about one, then. Not Toby."

"Well, I met this girl in California. Her name was Audrey, she was going to Berkeley—"

"Stop!" Finn clapped her hands over her ears. "Don't tell me!" She was starting to feel bad thinking about other girls Seth had loved.

He took her hands. "You're really acting funny today."

"I don't know what you mean. I'm not the one boasting about all the boys I've known!"

"Boasting," he said. "You asked me."

"Well," she said stubbornly, "you brought up the

subject." Then she saw the time on his watch. "Seth! I've got to run. I'll miss my bus."

They ran down the creaky stairs past the skinny lady and out into the street. "Come again," she called, as Finn turned back to pull the big door shut. "It's so nice to have young people take an interest."

At the bus stop Seth held Finn's hand. "I didn't mean to upset you. Those other girls—there weren't that many, Finn." He squeezed her hand. "Besides, not one compared to you."

"You liar!" she said, laughing.

"No, I mean it," he called as she got on the bus. She sat down and waved to him from the window. Even if what he said about her wasn't one hundred percent true, it made her feel good, more fuel for the little oven that glowed inside her whenever she was with Seth. Even after the bus had gone far down the street and she couldn't see him anymore, what he'd said went on warming her.

16

"Is this the girl in the long green coat that comes in all the time?" Mr. Hagen said. "The girl who's always calling?"

Finn shifted the phone to her other ear. "Yes . . ." she said. "I have a green coat." She glanced at William behind the counter.

"Don't call him here anymore."

"What?"

"Don't call. Don't come into my place. You hear me?"

She nodded. "Thank you," she said. She was so shaken, she said thank you to Mr. Hitler Hagen. She sat down at a table. The floor was damp. Outside the streets were running with water. Overnight the temperature had soared, and the snow was disappearing.

"Want something, Finn?" William said.

"Yes, sure," she said. Did Mr. Hagen hate anybody

who was young, and happy, and in love? And now what? How was she going to see Seth? It was Friday. He worked all weekend. How was she even going to get in touch with him if she couldn't call Maggie's and couldn't call the Apple?

"Cheer up," William said, sliding the pizza across to her. "Better days are coming. Uncle William says so."

She made herself smile. "I guess Uncle William knows."

When she got home, her father was in the kitchen sorting the mess in the fishing box. "Hi, honey. Look at this." He held up a little silver minnow. "This is going to get me the big one, Finn. A real lunker."

"I hope so, Dad." She was still upset over Mr. Hagen's ultimatum. She wanted to go in her room and think.

"This morning your mom said all that water running makes her feel like spring is really on the way." Every year her parents trout-fished in Catherine Creek. "You want to come with us this year? I'll get you a pair of waders."

"Oh . . . maybe," she said, moving past him. Her father's being so nice only made her feel worse. Her parents never said anything about Seth anymore. But Finn knew they were watching her. For a while now her father would be working in the area, going out in the morning, coming back at night.

"My dream come true," her mother said. "We're regular people." They all ate supper together, watched TV, got up in the morning, and ate breakfast at the same time. It was nice, but it also meant two pairs of eyes and two pairs of ears constantly on Finn. Whenever she went out, someone wanted to know where, who with, for how long, and when would she be home.

Sometimes she got so sick of lying that she would imagine just point-blank telling them the truth. *I've been with Seth . . . I'm going to meet Seth . . . Seth, Seth, Seth . . .* Say his name loud and clear, make them listen, make them understand. *She was seeing Seth.*

The weekend dragged. Everytime the phone rang, Finn was torn between hoping it was Seth and dreading that it was. A couple of times she was almost sure it must have been him, because when her mother answered, whoever it was hung up.

"Crank calls," her mother said. "We seem to have had a rash of them lately."

It wasn't till Monday after school that Finn got downtown. Outside the Apple she stood in front of the plate-glass window until Seth noticed her. He motioned her to come inside. She shook her head and pointed back of the building. Then she went around and waited for him there. There were three big green garbage loaders in back, and mounds of melting, filthy snow.

"Finn—" Seth was at the back door. "Come on in!"

"I can't. Your boss won't let me." She told him about the phone call with Mr. Hagen.

"That ass!" He came outside and closed the door behind him. "Him and his crummy job. You never did anything wrong, and he's got no complaints about my work. It would serve him right if I quit."

She put her hand on his arm. "Seth, you don't want to quit—"

"Oh, no?" He grinned at her. "C'mere." They stood together against the building, kissing. They had become very close, brought together by her parents' opposition and even closer by Maggie's. Having to be so careful, talking everything over together, and figuring out ways of seeing each other without anyone knowing, bound them together like two soldiers in a war. Her parents, her sister, and his brother were the enemy. And in this war Finn and Seth were both friends and comrades. And even more, Finn thought, her hand against the back of Seth's neck, because they were in love.

Finally, breathless, they broke apart, looked at each other, smiled ruefully. He gave her a little hug. "Listen, I've got to go in now. Don't worry about anything. I'll call you."

"My father's home for a while. He's working out of the office here."

"Yeeee!" Seth pulled at his hair. "Hagen! Your father! Your mother! Your sister! My brother!"

"I know," she said, half laughing, "it's awful, isn't it?"

They agreed to meet on his lunch hour Saturday at the library. There was nothing else they could do. But on Wednesday when Finn came out of school, Seth was waiting for her, leaning against a tree, arms folded, and looking very pleased with himself.

"I quit the job!"

"You didn't, Seth."

"Told you I would." He took some of her books. "You should have seen Hagen's face." He put his free arm around her. They stood against a tree, kissing. A car full of boys passed. "Way to go, lovers," the boys yelled.

The sun was out, the snow was going fast. You could

actually walk on the sidewalks. "Let's go someplace nice," Seth said. "Celebrate my liberation."

"How about celebrating with an ice cream soda," Finn said. "I haven't had a soda in ages."

"I wasn't thinking of food. I was thinking more along the lines of going up to the apartment."

"Maggie's place?" He nodded. "Seth, I can't."

"You won't see her. She's at work, and Jim's at the library."

"Can we buy something to eat on the way?"

"Is food ever far from your mind!"

"Creep." She shoved him, then ran away before he could shove back.

They stopped in a market and bought milk, cheese, crackers, and a giant Hershey bar. Standing in line with their stuff, Finn wondered if the lady behind her thought they were married. Keeping her hands in front of her she slipped off all her rings but one on the fourth finger of her left hand.

At Maggie's apartment they went into the kitchen and started eating. Finn made herself a cheese, chocolate, and cracker sandwich. "Are you kidding?" Seth said. "Cheese and chocolate?" He tipped back in his chair. "I've got to hit all the junk-food joints again for a job. A factory job would be better, though—big bucks."

They cleaned up and put away the food. In the living room Seth put on a Joni Mitchell record and they danced and kissed. Then they fell into a chair and kissed some more. Finn sat on his lap with her legs dangling over the side of the chair. Seth unsnapped her jeans and put his hand on her belly and then inside her pants. She pushed her face into his neck.

"Like it . . . ?"

"Yes . . ."

There were steps in the hall. Finn jumped up and ran into the kitchen, pulling her clothes together. The door opened. "Seth," she heard Jim say, "you're home early."

"Quit my job," Seth answered.

"Quit. What for?"

Finn knew she had to go out there and say hello to Jim. Her throat was dry. She ran a glass of water and walked into the living room. "Hi, Jim."

He put down his briefcase. He was wearing a corduroy jacket and a plaid vest. "What are you doing here, Finn?"

"I invited Finn here," Seth said.

Jim took off his glasses and polished them on a hankie. "It's my understanding that you two aren't supposed to see each other."

Finn sipped her water, unable to think of a thing to say. She and Seth looked at each other. Seth shrugged.

"What the hell's going on?" Jim said. "Are you losing your grip, Seth? First you quit your job, then you bring Finn here."

"Look," Seth said tensely, "why don't you mind your own business."

"This is my business. How many times have you brought Finn here? I'm not going to be a party to—"

"You don't have to be a party to anything," Seth said.

"Don't be a horse's ass. This is my apartment—"

"Shove it!" Seth jumped up. "Shove your apartment!" He ran out the door, banging it behind him.

Finn scooped up her books and ran after Seth. Then she stopped. "Jim—don't tell my parents."

"You know how they feel, Finn. You're going behind their backs."

"I know!" she cried. "I know it! You and Maggie weren't always so perfect. Are you going to fink on me?"

Jim held up his hands. "All right. Don't worry."

Finn ran down the three flights and out to the street. Seth was almost out of sight. She called him, but he didn't stop. She ran and caught up with him halfway down the next block.

"Leave me alone, Finn."

"But—"

"I said leave me alone."

"I just want to help you."

"Please—bug off!"

She stopped short. "Well, dammit, the same to you!" She crossed the street. He didn't call her back. A bus was just pulling up at the stop. She got on. "Nice day," the driver said as she dropped her token in.

She took a seat. There was the most awful feeling in her chest. The bus rumbled down the street. Through the window she saw Seth walking rapidly, his head down. Only minutes ago they'd been sitting in a chair, their arms around each other. Close, so close. And now she felt so distant from him. Hurting and distant. The bus passed him, and she thought, What if that's the last time I ever see him?

17

"I still don't see why you quarreled," Vida said. "It must have had something to do with sex. Did he want something you—"

"Look, Vida, you've got the wrong impression," Finn said. "A lot of things happened, but not the thing you're thinking of."

"You mean you haven't?"

"Haven't what?" Finn was short tempered.

"Come on," Vida said. "Did you or didn't you?"

"Didn't." Why did making love have to mean just what you finally did? Crazy. Everything was crazy. Her fight with Seth. This conversation with Vida. The craziest thing of all was that she and Seth hadn't fought over anything.

That's what she wanted to tell Seth. We had a fight, and you're not even mad at *me*!

On her lunch hour she went out of school and over

to the pizzeria. She debated calling the Apple on the chance Seth might answer the phone, then remembered he'd quit his job. Okay, that meant he was home. She dialed Maggie's. "Hello? Maggie here."

Without answering Finn hung up.

Friday night, late, Finn had just finished brushing her teeth when the phone rang. "Finn, answer it," her mother called from her bedroom.

"Hello—"

"Finn. Is that you?" Seth said.

She held the phone tightly against her ear. His voice . . . his voice, which she had thought she might never hear again. Wednesday. Wednesday night. Thursday. Thursday night. Friday. Now it was Friday night. All that time . . . all those hours . . . the injustice of it . . . that he had turned on her. . . .

"Yes, it's me." The house was dark except for the faint spill of light coming from under her parents' closed door.

"Hello—I can't hear you very well."

"You shouldn't have called here."

"I know. I would have hung up if anybody else— listen I want to talk to you. I want to see you."

She waited a moment. "So you can tell me to bug off?"

"No, I'm sorry about that. You know I didn't mean it. Tomorrow? Can we meet tomorrow? What's a good place for you?"

Again she waited. Her throat was tight. The hurt hadn't gone away just because he'd called. "Nick's

Pizzeria," she said finally. "Near my school. Do you know where it is?"

"I'll find it. What time?"

She glanced down the hall at her parents' room. "Two o'clock."

"Not earlier?"

"I have to help my mother clean the house."

"All right. Two o'clock. Finn . . . I love you."

She wanted to say it back. She knew he was waiting. But she couldn't—not this time.

"Who was that?" her mother called from her room as Finn went past.

"No one. Just a kid from school."

"Open the door. I can't hear you."

Reluctantly Finn opened their door a crack. There was a little light from their radio. "Tell your friends not to call so late," her father said. She could just make out his bulk.

"I'm sorry. I will."

"It wasn't Vida, was it?" her mother said.

"No, not Vida." Finn's hands were damp. "It was, ah, Beth," she said, hearing the resemblance to Seth too late.

In the morning she worked side by side with her mother, vacuuming, washing woodwork and windows, and polishing silver. After they finished, she showered and then got dressed. She left her hair loose and wore a gray, full skirt and a soft, pink blouse. Over that, her yellow slicker.

Her parents were in the kitchen having lunch. "I

wish you wouldn't smoke when you eat," her mother was saying.

Her father put out his cigarette. "How's that?"

"Nice," Finn's mother said. They leaned toward each other and kissed.

"I'm going out," Finn said. "Downtown with Vida. Maybe we'll go to a movie."

"What time will you be home?" her father asked.

"I don't know, about five, I suppose."

"Okay, have fun," her father said.

She stopped in to Vida's and told her the plan. Vida was going downtown, as it turned out. "Wish you'd give me some warning, though," she said, hurrying to get dressed.

"I told you, Vida, I couldn't. He called too late last night, and this morning Mom didn't leave me alone for a second."

It was raining when they went out. Finn walked to the bus stop with Vida. "Five o'clock, right?" Vida said.

"Good," Finn said. She pulled up the hood on her slicker. Part of her wanted to hurry, but part of her wanted Seth to get there first and have to wait for her.

Seth was sitting at a corner table in Nick's. He was wearing jeans, a denim shirt. His hands were in his jacket pockets. When he saw her, he pushed back his chair. "Hi. You're here."

She nodded. "I'm here." She didn't meet his eyes.

"So how are you? Sit down."

She sat stiffly. She couldn't stop thinking how he'd told her to bug off. How could he have done a thing like that if he loved her?

"Finn, are you still mad at me?" he said.

"Why should I be?" she said with an artificial laugh.

"I acted rotten to you."

"Yes, you did." She looked at him. "You were mad at your brother, and you took it out on me."

"I know," he said.

"That was so unfair!"

"I know," he said again. "I'm really sorry. It was punky, a punky thing to do."

Four girls came in. Finn knew a couple of them. They stared at Seth. "Hi, Finn."

She forced a smile. "Hi, Mitzi. Hi, Wendy." She turned her chair so her back was to them. Seth reached for her hand.

"Don't!" She pulled her hand away. She was afraid she was going to cry. She felt so mixed-up—furious at him for having been mean to her, and yet at the same time sorry for him because he looked sad.

"It's unfair of you to look like that," she said fiercely, keeping her voice down.

"I don't know what you mean. I just want to make up. . . ."

"*That's* what I mean!" A tear slid out of one eye. "*Don't* be so nice!"

"What do I have to say?"

"Nothing! You don't have to say anything," she choked.

"Finn, don't cry." He took her hand. In the midst of her crazy misery she shivered voluptuously at the warmth of his hand on hers. "What happened had nothing to do with you. I was out of control. You know that, don't you?" She shook her head, pressing her lips together to keep back the tears. "Jesus, that was just totally unfair of me," he said.

"Yes . . . it was. . . ."

"You're my friend."

"Am I?"

"Don't say that, please. You know you are." He rubbed her fingers, warming them. "Your hands are icy." She felt herself giving way, felt the hurt and anger leaving.

He pulled his chair around next to hers and put his arm around her. "Honey . . . is it okay?"

She nodded, biting her lip. "It's . . . okay."

"Really?"

"Really," she said.

He squeezed her and kissed her cheek. "I'm glad. You had me worried! Wow. Now I'm hungry. Let's have a pizza. You want a pizza? I do!" He went to the counter to order. "What do you want, Finn?" he called. "Cheese? Or cheese and sausage?"

"You choose," she said, wiping her eyes with a napkin.

"No, you. Your choice," he said. "I don't care."

"I don't, either."

"How about it, you two," William said. "Cheese and sausage, right?"

"That's it, man," Seth said.

Finn leaned on her hand, watching him. She loved looking at him. She loved him again. It made her feel wonderful, it was an incredible feeling. Almost in a moment her misery had gone, and she was happy again.

Seth came back to the table, carrying the pizza on a tin tray. He sat down. Now she pulled her chair closer to his. Their legs touched. "Hey, you need a haircut," she said, ruffling his hair. She wanted to touch him.

She looked around. Everything seemed different now. The girls hunched over their Cokes, William, the signs on the walls—all of it seemed somehow different—wonderful.

Seth doubled over a slice of pizza. "I've got things to tell you. I've been busy. I've got a job, and that's not all. I've found a room, too. I slept downtown at the Y Wednesday night. I wasn't going back to Jim's. I would've slept in the street first."

"I can't believe we had our first fight," Finn said. "I didn't think we'd ever fight."

"Everyone does," Seth said.

When they left, it was raining harder than before. The wind was blowing the tree branches around. Signs creaked on their poles. They took a bus to Tar Street, where Seth had rented an attic room in a big old unpainted frame house that had seen its best days. Three flights of thinly roofed dilapidated stairs ran up one side of the building.

The wooden railing shook beneath her hand. She looked down into the bare yard. "Seth, you didn't tell me where you found a job."

"Potato chip factory." At the head of the stairs he unlocked a door. There was barely room enough for both of them on the landing. He stepped inside, switched on an overhead light, and waited for Finn to enter. "Well, what do you think?"

The walls sloped, the rafters were bare and dusty. "It's really an attic," she said. There was a bed and a bureau, a fat red armchair with stuffing spilling out, and in a partitioned-off area, a kitchen—sink, stove, fridge, and a table and two chairs.

Seth hung his jacket on a hook on the wall and held out his hand for Finn's raincoat. She went to the window and looked down at the street. "It's nice being up so high."

"I was lucky to get this place." He touched her shoulder. "Your shirt's damp." He pulled a shirt out of the bureau. "Want to put this on? I went over to Jim's yesterday when he and Maggie were out and took all my stuff."

"What do you do about a bathroom?" she said.

He pointed to the kitchen section. "There's a john just past that."

Finn turned her back and changed shirts. "You're not wearing a bra," he said.

"I don't all the time." She put her damp shirt on the hot-air vent. She sat down on the bed and bounced up and down. The mattress was lumpy. The bed was nice, though. It had four wooden posts carved in the form of pineapples and it was covered with a patched blue-and-red quilt. "Where does all this stuff come from?" Finn said.

"It goes with the place, except the quilt is mine."

"Is this room very expensive?"

"Not that bad," he said. "It's worth every cent to me."

She walked around the room, looking at everything. In the kitchen, a shelf held a small array of canned goods, a few dishes and cups, and a handful of silverware in a pitcher. Finn opened the refrigerator. "Don't tell me you're hungry again," Seth said.

"Just checking up. Are you really working in a potato chip factory? I thought potato chips grew on potato chip trees."

"Right. And next to them are the Coca-Cola trees. You know Flips Chips?"

"Everyone knows Flips Chips."

"Well, you are now speaking to an official Flips Chips chip-maker. I start work Monday." He put his arms around her and they stood in the middle of the room, holding each other and kissing. "Let's lie down on the bed," he said.

"The bed?"

"It's big enough for both of us."

"That's not what I'm worried about."

"You don't have to worry about anything," he said. He took off his boots and lay down, pulling the quilt up to his chin. "See?" He smiled at her. "Nothing to it. "Come on in."

She sat down next to him. "I don't think I will, Seth."

"What are you afraid of?" he said.

"Nothing. I just don't think it's a very good idea."

"You're wrong. It's a great idea. What's the big deal?"

She was starting to feel a little foolish. "I don't know. It's just—it's a bed."

"So?" he said.

"So, beds are where people make love."

"So?" he said again.

"So, I told you how I felt about that."

"Look, if you don't want anything to happen, nothing is going to happen." He pulled her toward him. "It's nicer here than in the movies or the museum."

She slid down next to him. He was right—whatever they were going to do was up to them. It wasn't where you were that mattered, but what you had on your mind.

They turned so they were facing each other. He pulled the quilt over her. "My grandmother made this quilt for me. I've had it forever."

"Lucky," she said.

They kissed . . . they embraced and snuggled closer to each other. "This is nice," he said. "Isn't it nice?"

She nodded. It *was* nice, and exciting and a little scary, but cozy, too. The rain drummed on the roof.

Seth unbuttoned her shirt. He took off his jeans. She took off her skirt. They pressed close and kissed for a long time. She felt a kind of sweet aching in her stomach. She was feeling everything in her stomach. "Touch me?" he said.

"Yes . . ." She'd been away somewhere, in another world. "You're pretty," she said.

"What?" He laughed.

"You—your skin, everything. Pretty."

He hugged her to him. "I like you," he said. "I like you, Finn Rousseau. I like your name, I like your face, I like you!" Then he said, "Oh!" and then, "Oh!" again, and turned quickly away. "I'm coming!" he cried.

She put her hand on his back. She felt him trembling. A tenderness grew in her . . . as if she wanted to put out wings and cover him. A glowy feeling, like mist, spread through her, reaching from her center outward. She loved him. She stroked his hair, his back.

He was quiet. "Are you all right?" she said.

He turned back toward her. "I'm happy," he said. He put his hand against her cheek. "How about you?"

"I'm good," she said. "Very good."

"I didn't mean that to happen. I couldn't help it."

"I didn't mind," she said. "I liked it."

They lay together quietly. A streak of light came through the window. "It's clearing," she said.

"You know what I'm thinking," Seth said. "If I had a car, we'd get in and just drive off. We'd drive away together and keep going to wherever the road led us."

"What would we do when we ran out of gas?"

"Oh . . . stop and look around. See if we liked where we were. And if we did, we'd rent a room just like this."

"Yes," she said, smiling. "An attic room."

"We'd find jobs," Seth said, "and—"

"Buy food."

"You'd be in charge of that," he said, "I'd be in charge of the laundry."

"All right," she said. "We'll do the dishes together after we eat. And you can teach me to drive."

"Right. We'll read books together, go to the movies, and take long walks."

"It sounds nice," she said.

"We'd share a bed."

"Cuddle. And kiss all the time."

He laughed. "Okay. And maybe we'll do some other things, too."

She snuggled closer. "We'd really be friends, wouldn't we?"

"Good friends," he said.

"Best friends," she said.

"Best friends," he agreed. "Better than best friends."

She was so happy. She thought, This is what love really is. And if, at that moment, a fairy godmother had appeared to give her three wishes, Finn would have had only one—to stay like that with Seth in his attic room forever. No, not to stay there, but to feel that way—happy, contented, trusting and loving—forever.

18

"Where've you been?" her father said, reaching for a cigarette, but not lighting it.

Finn looked up at the clock. Seven o'clock. She'd known it was late when she left Seth's room, but not this late.

"I thought you were with Vida," her mother said.

"Yes," she said.

"Vida got home hours ago."

The table was set for three. They had eaten. Her plate was sitting there, untouched. "I'm sorry I'm so late."

"Where were you?" her father said. He held up his hand. "And don't tell us you were with Vida."

It was incredible the way her heart was banging inside her chest. She thought of all kinds of things to say. Lies. More lies. *I was with a friend. . . . I was alone. . . . I was with Vida, she just went home early. . . .*

"I was with Seth," she said. She took off her raincoat and hung it over a chair. How many times she had wanted to say his name in just that way—simply, directly, without evasion.

"Seth?" her mother said.

"Yes," she said, and repeated it, "Seth." The sense of relief, for the moment, was overwhelming.

"Not—*Beth*?" Her mother had caught that.

"How long have you been seeing him?" her father said, scraping back his chair. "This isn't the first time."

"No. Not the first time." She couldn't stop her heart's fearful pounding.

"How long?" her father said again, moving toward her.

"For . . . a while."

"What does that mean, Finn?" He took her by the shoulder. "Ever since we told you not to?"

"Dad—"

He shook her. "Ted," her mother said.

"Yes or no, Finn?" her father said.

"Yes."

"Yes, you've been seeing him ever since we told you not to?"

"Yes."

"Well, what the hell is going on between you two?"

"Nothing! Dad, you're hurting me." She twisted away.

"Nothing," her mother said. "Is that all you have to say, Finn?"

"What do you want me to say?" She felt cornered. "Do you want me to tell you about every kiss we had?"

"Stop yelling!" her father said. "We're not interested in kissing."

"Daddy—"

"Don't you 'Daddy' me, Finn."

Tears came to her eyes. She couldn't hold them back. "You don't let me pick my own friends." Her voice was wobbling. It infuriated her. "It's not right. I'm a person. You can't tell me everything to do or not do."

"We leave plenty of things up to you," her mother said.

"Sure!" Finn turned on her mother. It was always easier to be mad at her mother than at her father. "What to wear to school, and if I want a hot or a cold breakfast!" She knew she was talking too fast, too loud. "I don't know what you want!" she exclaimed.

But the moment she said it, she thought of Seth's room where the two of them had been on his bed. That was what her parents meant. That was what they wanted to know. Were she and Seth having sex?

She opened her mouth to deny it, then set her lips. She couldn't . . . she wouldn't . . . tell them the personal things between her and Seth. It was private, it was personal, it was hers—hers and Seth's—and nobody else's.

"Didn't it ever bother you that you were lying to us?" her mother said.

"It bothered me."

"Bullshit!" Her father swore. "If it bothered you, you wouldn't have done it." Then he went into a real rage. "We're your parents, doesn't that mean one goddamned thing to you! If we tell you something, *you do it*!"

"No, that's not—" Finn began.

"No?" he repeated, interrupting her, and he reached over and slapped her.

Her hand went to her cheek. Rage filled her. "You told me not to see Seth, and I did anyway." She was shaking. "If you tell me the same thing again, I'll still see him. You can beat me up, and I'll still see him."

She ran out of the kitchen. In her room she waited for her father to come after her. She stood in the middle of the room, waiting and shaking. If he hit her again, she wouldn't cry. She'd hit him back. He had no right to hit her!

She heard her parents going out. She heard the car cough to life in the driveway downstairs. She listened till the sound of the car disappeared, then she sat down abruptly on her bed.

Where had they gone? What were they going to do? Lock her in her room? Tie her to her bed? Send her to reform school?

She made herself open her English book and do a page of homework. She wrote a sentence, stopped, her pen in midair. Everything she'd said, everything they'd said, repeated in her head. And again she felt her father's hand crack against her cheek.

Her parents came in late. Finn was glad. She didn't want to see them. But in the morning they were waiting for her when she got up. They had already eaten. They both sat at the kitchen table watching her peel an orange, make toast, drink a glass of milk. Her father smoked, her mother polished silverware.

Finn put her glass in the sink and started to walk out. "Hold it," her father said. She paused, not looking at him. "We're going to talk," he said. "Sit down."

"I don't want to talk to you. You hit me!"

"I didn't want to." His broad face was dark. "Don't you think it hurt me?"

"Oh, no! Don't say that! I don't believe that." She sat down as far away from him as possible.

"I want us all to talk like people," her mother said. "No screaming, no shouting. Finn, you first. What do you have to say?"

Finn touched her cheek. She shook her head. "Nothing."

"Nothing?" her father said.

"Now is your chance," her mother said. She waited a moment. "All right, then we'll tell you what we've decided. You're grounded for a month. You're not to see this boy. You're to come straight home from school. . . ."

"I won't," Finn said. The words were out without thought. There was a terrible feeling in her stomach. She felt almost nauseated.

"You won't?" Her father hit the table with his fist. "You won't?" he repeated.

Finn sucked in her breath. Jesus, don't let him hit me again, she thought. She had been hit very seldom in her life. The idea of her father's trying to force her to do something by beating her was terrible! It was the most horrible thing in the world to force someone else with physical strength.

Her mother and father were looking at her like two

strangers, cold and remote, so far removed from her that a wave of terror ran through Finn.

"I'm sorry . . . I'm really sorry . . . but I told you . . . I've got a right to see Seth . . . and if you hit me, it'll just be worse. . . ."

"I don't know you anymore," her father said in a strained voice. "I don't know either of my daughters anymore."

"Daddy, please . . . I'm not doing anything wrong."

He walked out of the kitchen. Her mother stood up. "Your father's terribly upset. He feels terrible. You know how much he thinks of you. It hurts him so much the way you're acting! And I'm not even speaking about the way I feel." She pulled her robe around her and went after Finn's father.

Finn felt dazed. After a while she went into her room. She was crying. She lay down on her bed and cried with her head under the pillow.

Later she took a shower. Standing under the hot water she went over everything again, everything they had said last night, everything they had said this morning. At least now they knew about Seth. Now they knew how she really felt. She didn't know what would happen next, but it would all be out in the open. No more secrets. Little by little she began to feel a bit better.

19

"I'll have ten fifteen-cent stamps, please," Finn said, pushing two dollar bills across the counter.

"Oh, you will, will you?" a familiar voice said lightly behind her.

Picking up her change and the stamps, she turned to see Maggie with a fistful of envelopes. Wearing a longish, full skirt, high leather boots, and a short fur coat, Maggie looked sophisticated and briskly fashionable. "Well," she said, smiling, "what a funny place to meet my sister."

But Finn, remembering the last time she'd talked to Maggie—nearly a month ago—didn't return the smile. Maggie took Finn's place in line. "Don't go," she said, waving the envelopes. "I'm just mailing these for my lawyers."

Finn felt awkward. She moved over to one of the high desks, fussing with her stamps and change to cover her confusion. Her footsteps echoed in the old marble-floored building.

"Finn, this is really good," Maggie said, coming over.

"I've been meaning to call you. Where's Seth? Jim has been damn worried."

Finn pushed through the glass door. "What's he worried about?"

"Are you kidding?" Maggie said. "Do you realize Seth just didn't come home one night? And the next morning all his things were gone. Pffft! Just like that, he disappears. How were we supposed to feel?"

"I don't know," Finn said. "I only know Jim acted pretty bad to Seth."

"Oh, you two kids—" Maggie began.

"Maggie," Finn interrupted, "If you want to talk to me, just don't put me down. All right? I mean, talk to me. Just talk to me like I'm someone, not a brainless juvenile."

"Whew, aren't you hot under the collar," Maggie said.

They stood on the corner, waiting for the light to change. Hot under the collar was exactly the right term for the way Finn felt. Standing there with Maggie, remembering how her sister had let her down, and realizing how much their relationship had changed, Finn felt a wave of heat rising from her neck to her forehead.

She crossed the street fast, a step ahead of Maggie.

Maggie put out her hand to hold Finn back. "Would you at least tell me where Seth is?"

"No," Finn said. "I'm not going to. I don't know if Seth wants Jim to know."

They stood there, looking at each other. Maggie sighed. "How does everything get so complicated?" She shifted from foot to foot, and the impression of a controlled young career-woman faded. She looked troubled.

Finn felt the heat in her face ebbing. They'd been friends once—when Maggie still lived at home. When Finn was Maggie's adoring younger sister. Now everything had changed. As Maggie said, become more complicated.

Maggie glanced at the clock in front of the jewelers'. "I better get back to the office. Walk with me, okay? I'm in The Hendley-Simpson Building." The streets were slushy. A raw wind blew between the buildings.

"I hear things between you and Mom and Dad are rough right now," Maggie said. "I hear there was a big blowup last week."

"Yes," Finn said, "there was almost as big a fight as when you moved out."

"Mom sounded pretty down when I talked to her."

"Mom!" Finn said. "She didn't get her face slapped."

"Rough as that?" Maggie said.

"Yes," Finn said. "You moved out, but I can't do that."

"I hope not!" Maggie said. She turned to look at Finn. "You're not thinking of anything stupid like that, are you? You shouldn't compare yourself to me, Finn. I'm much older than you."

Finn hunched against the wind. "I know that, Maggie! I know a lot more than you, or Mom, or Dad give me credit for."

"Don't be so touchy," Maggie said. "Here's my building. Come on in for a minute." They went up a short flight of stairs into the lobby.

"I'm on the fourth floor," Maggie said, pushing the button for the elevator. The doors slid open, but Maggie ignored it and pulled Finn to one side. "Listen," she said, "Mom and Dad aside, don't get too involved with Seth. He's got his own problems. He's not quite the sweetheart he seems at first. And you're awfully young. Now, don't take offense! I can just see you want to tell me off—"

"Yes, I'm so sick of hearing how young I am."

"Well, it's true enough, Finn. Believe me, that was what was really on my mind when I told you right in the beginning to go along with Mom and Dad."

Finn met her sister's eyes. "Let's not go over all that again."

"If that's the way you want it," Maggie said.

"It is."

Maggie pulled off her fur hat. Her curls sprang out. "Well, anyway, will you tell Seth that Jim would like to hear from him?"

"Yes," Finn said, "I'll do that."

"Okay, thanks," Maggie said. She got into the elevator. Finn waved and walked toward the door. Finally she was pleased with the way things had gone. Maggie had dropped her older-sister pose at the end and just spoken to Finn like another person. Good, Finn thought. Good!

A few days later Finn waited for Seth outside the factory. They were closing early for inventory. She and

Seth had not seen each other since the afternoon in his room. Finn was treading carefully at home. Things were, as Maggie had rightly said, rough, and every time she came in even a few minutes late, the tension went up another notch.

Finn drew in a deep breath of air. The sky was wet, a silky April sky. Gray clouds blew over. It was so good to be out, to breathe the air, and not to feel the hard looks of her parents.

In a few moments Seth came out with his knapsack slung over his shoulder. He put her books into his sack. "Well, they're counting the potato chips," he said. He took her hand. "Hi."

"Hi." They smiled at each other.

"Let's go to my room. I've been painting it. Wait till you see."

"I've got to be home on time, or my parents—"

"Sure, don't worry," he said, cracking thin ice on a puddle. "Things still bad?"

Finn nodded. "It's so ugly, Seth."

He squeezed her hand. "I wish I could do something."

"You can't."

"Well, if we didn't see each other—"

"Seth." She was stricken. She stopped walking. "Do you mean that? You don't mean it, do you?"

He laughed at her. "I'm just teasing, baby. Can't you tell when I'm teasing?"

"Ugh," she said, pushing him away. "Don't tease about important things."

As they were going up the stairs to his room, she

remembered her meeting with Maggie, and told him about it. "Jim wants to hear from you," she said. "I guess he's worried or something."

Seth nodded. "I'll give him a ring. I meant to do it, anyway."

"So your fight is over just like that?" Finn said.

"Well—" Seth shrugged. "We've had so many."

Seth had been working on his room. There was a poster tacked on one of the slanting walls showing a little farmhouse snuggled in a valley. There was a stack of books on the floor near the bed, blueberry jelly and bread on the table, and a bunch of bittersweet stuck into an empty jar.

One wall had been painted a dark green. "It looks nice," Finn said.

"I'm doing this wall a lighter green," Seth said. "Sort of like the color of that coat you were wearing this winter." He poured paint into a pan, dipped in a roller, and made a wide swath down one wall.

"That's not my coat color," Finn said. "That's the color of avocados."

"You like it?"

"Do some more." She stood back. "Yes, it's really great."

"Help yourself to food," he said.

She fixed a jelly sandwich and ate it, looking out the window. "I just had some really bad news about Paul and Vida. They're breaking up."

"How come?" he said.

"They had a fight over strawberries."

He stopped painting and looked at her. "Come on. How can anybody fight over strawberries?"

"Well, last night Paul was going to eat supper with Vida's family, and Paul and Vida were going to make strawberry shortcake to surprise everyone. Whipped cream, the whole deal. Vida wanted to buy fresh strawberries—"

"The best kind," Seth put in.

"—but Paul said no, they were too expensive, they should get frozen strawberries. They got into this big fight, and that was it."

"You're not kidding me?"

"I know it sounds dumb," Finn said. "I guess the strawberries didn't actually have that much to do with it. It was really an excuse for breaking up. Vida said it's been coming for a long time."

"It doesn't sound like they had that much going for them," Seth said, dipping the roller into the pan again.

"No, they really did. They were together for a long time. They were sleeping together."

Seth looked over at her. "She does, but you don't. I thought she was your best girl friend."

"Vida and I don't look at everything the same way," Finn said. "That doesn't stop us from being friends," she added pointedly.

"I get the message." He came over and kissed her. "You taste like blueberry jam."

"You smell like avocado paint." She liked how soft his mouth was. He nudged her toward the bed. "Let's fool around," he said.

"No, really, Seth, I've got to go in five minutes. Well, ten, anyway."

"You should see what I can do in ten minutes." He twirled an imaginary mustache.

"Some other time, thanks."

"Tell me, my pretty one, how do you feel about new experiences?" he said.

"Just fine."

"Experience for the sake of experience?"

"Uh-uh." She leaned back against his arms. He had paint on his hands and was being careful not to touch her with them.

"Very narrow-minded," he said. "You gotta try everything at least once before you make up your mind."

"I don't have to drink poison even once to find out what I think about it," she said.

"Poison? Is that what you think sex is?"

"No, that's what you are," she said, laughing. "Pretty poison!"

"I'll get you for that," he said.

"When?" she said, pulling back.

He locked his hands behind her. "Right now." He kissed her neck, then licked it.

"That tickles!"

"Say you love me," he ordered.

"I love you."

"Say 'I'm yours.' "

"I'm mine," she said, grinning.

"Say 'I'd do anything for you.' "

"I'd do anything for you—almost."

"Say 'I'm Seth's.' "

"I'm Finn's."

"Come on, stingy! Say it."

"Uh-uh."

He wrapped his arms tighter around her. "Say it. Say 'I'm Seth's.' "

"Hey! I can't breathe. Loosen up."

"Say it. Say Uncle."

"Let me go first." She freed one hand and punched him in the belly.

"Oooh! You hurt me." He bent over, holding his arms around himself.

"Seth? Are you really hurting?"

He looked up, then grabbed her again. "Ha-ha! Fooled you." When she tried to squirm free, he caught her by the seat of her pants. "Now I've put my mark on you," he said.

She looked over her shoulder. "You creep." There were two pale green handprints on her pants. "What am I going to tell my mother?"

He started to laugh. "The green cookie monster got sexy."

"Very funny. What am I going to do now?" She pushed him away. "That was so juvenile!"

"Ha! Talk about juvenile. Don't you think your ideas about sex are a little, little juvenile also?"

"You really are crazy today," she said. "What's sex got to do with ruining my pants?"

"You didn't cooperate, remember? Maybe you think I don't have the finest techniques of lovemaking—"

"I wouldn't know a fine technique if I fell over it."

"True. You're a sexual ignoramus."

"I suppose you know everything!"

"Yes. And I'm willing to teach it all to you. I want you to get over these foolish ideas you have about virginity."

"My ideas are about making love. About when I will do it. You make what I feel sound like a disease."

"It is. It's making me sick." He held his stomach. "Can't you see how I'm suffering?"

"How am I going to get this paint out?"

"It'll wash off. Just take off your jeans—"

"Oh-ho, now I get it."

"I promise not to look," he said.

"I bet!"

"No, I really mean it." He was grinning.

"Come on, Seth, be serious—"

"What fun is that?"

She couldn't help laughing. "Turn your back," she ordered. "Start painting again!" She handed him the roller. Then she took off her jeans and wrapped herself in a blanket.

"I can't believe how modest you are," he said, rolling the wall next to the window. "I've seen your underpants before."

"I know . . ." She washed out her jeans in the sink and put them over the vent to dry. "But this is different."

"Why?"

"You know . . . we were on the bed before . . ."

"You remember?" he asked, turning, the roller in the air.

"What do you think? Of course."

"It was nice, wasn't it?" Paint dripped on the floor.

"Yes, very." She felt shy talking about it. It was easier to joke about sex.

"Don't you want to do that again?" He set the roller in the pan and held out his hand.

"Seth . . . I can't now . . . I told you . . ." She leaned against him, her face near his.

"But we will again?"

"Yes," she said against his shirt. There was that aching sweetness spreading through her. They kissed. A very soft long kiss. "Oh . . ." For a few minutes Finn forgot everything. The squeal of brakes down in the street brought her back to herself.

"Seth, I'll be murdered if I don't get home on time." She ran to the vent for her jeans. They were still damp, but she put them on. "Have I got everything?" she said, taking her books out of his knapsack.

"When will we see each other again?" he asked.

"I don't know! My father's always around now."

"Isn't he going to do any long-distance hauling anymore?"

Finn shrugged. "My mother likes it this way. I think he does, too."

"Saturday I'll be busy," Seth said, "but maybe you could come here Sunday?"

"That would be nice! I'll try," she said.

Seth walked to the door with her. "I'll go down the stairs with you," he said. But downstairs he said he'd walk her to the corner, and then at the corner he kept going all the way to the bus stop.

"You're really crazy," she said happily.

20

Sunday morning Finn woke up thinking about Seth and wanting to see him. She had seen less of Seth these past few weeks than in all the time she'd known him. Her father was home, though, and so was her mother. It would be impossible to get out without either lying or fighting.

Punching her pillow, she remembered her big bold statements. *I won't be grounded. . . . I will see Seth.* . . . But the fact was, she might as well be grounded. She had been doing things her parents' way: coming home before they did, carefully letting them know where she was going and when she'd be back, and most of all, *not seeing Seth.* Since the big fight with her parents she had seen Seth just once, the other day in his room, and even then she had run home like a rabbit, fearful of being late.

She lay in bed for a long time, not wanting to get up

or do anything. Through her window she saw the sky, blue for a change! It was horrible being depressed on a day like this.

She made herself get up. She had homework to do, she could clean her room, take a walk with Vida, or any number of things. In the kitchen, her parents' breakfast dishes were in the sink. "Nice," Finn muttered. "Very nice. You made breakfast and didn't invite me." She could hear them talking in their bedroom.

She pushed bread into the toaster and broke two eggs into a frying pan. She dumped pepper on the eggs, wondering if Seth, too, was making his breakfast now. Was he waiting for her?

She sat down with her food, pushing her fork into the egg yolks. Seth was expecting her. She was sure of it. She half rose from the table, pushing away the uneaten eggs. She was a prisoner! So scared of her parents' disapproval, she didn't dare make a move.

She shoved her dishes into the sink. Defying her parents, she had felt independent, brave, grown-up! "What a joke," she said furiously. It had meant nothing.

She went into her room and dressed. She put on a light, flowered blouse and a string of pale yellow beads. She combed her hair, pulling it back with a big barrette, and put on all her silver rings. "Put on some silver . . ." she hummed, but she couldn't remember the rest of the words. "Nervous . . . I'm nervous. . . . Okay, I'm nervous." She was going out. She was going to see Seth. She didn't know what she would tell her parents.

She walked down the hall. "I'm off," she called through the door of her parents.

"Where are you going?" her mother called back.

"Out." Brilliant. She knew, they wouldn't fall for that.

"Come in here for a moment." That was her father. He and her mother were sprawled on top of their bed, still in their night clothes. Her mother was putting snapshots into an album, while her father was reading to her from the Sunday paper.

Finn stood in the doorway.

"Did you have breakfast?" her mother said. Finn nodded. "You're all dressed up. Where'd you say you were going?"

"I didn't."

"Well, say, then," her father said. His thick head of hair was unruly. He hadn't shaved yet. He was wearing blue-and-white-striped pajamas.

Finn's neck got hot. Here it was. She could lie to them, tell them a story, make up something. It wouldn't be hard. *I'm going for a walk . . . Vida and I are going to visit Paul . . .* the old stuff. Or she could tell them the truth.

"Do you want the truth, or a lie?" she said.

Her mother, holding a snapshot to the light, paused and looked at Finn. "The truth, please!"

Now they were both looking at her. She wiped her hands down the sides of her slacks. What had she done?

"Well?" her mother said.

"I'm going to see Seth." Her voice wobbled. "Okay, can I go?" She made paws in front of herself. Begging paws. It disgusted her.

"Are you asking us, or telling us?" her father said.

"I'm . . . asking," Finn said.

"Then the answer is no."

"Catch twenty-two," she exclaimed bitterly. "If I'd lied to you, it would have been okay. I would have gone out. But since I'm telling you the truth, you're punishing me!"

"You're missing the point—" her mother began.

"No, you are," Finn said heatedly. "Don't you see that you're making me lie?"

"No one can make you lie," her father said. He sat up, rolling a section of newspaper in his hand.

"If I want to see Seth, you've made it clear—I have to lie. *And I want to see him!*"

"*And we*," her father said, tapping the rolled up newspaper into the palm of his hand with each word, "*don't want you to see him.*"

"Dad," Finn cried, anguished. "Please . . ." She choked, she couldn't go on. What was the use? It was the same thing all over again. She wound her beads round and round her fingers. She wanted to scream, shout, throw something. She stood there, winding her beads, then letting them unwind, then winding them up again.

She and her parents were like two enemy tribes, wearing their animal skins and waving their spears at each other. Shouting across a chasm ten miles wide. She heard them, and they heard her, but neither one understood what the other was saying.

"If I told you I was going out to see Jerry Demas, I bet you wouldn't put all this heat on me."

"Who's Jerry Demas?" her mother said.

"A boy in school. He was at the New Year's Eve party I went to. He walked me home."

"How old is he?"

"I don't know, sixteen, I guess. Maybe seventeen."

"You're right," her father said. "We wouldn't put heat on you for that."

"*Why?*"

"Finn, you know why," her father said. He sighed. "Who he is, his age."

Finn drummed her fingers on the door. "Listen. Listen! You're so wrong. You don't realize—you think age is everything. You don't even know Jerry. He's a lot more . . . *dangerous* than Seth."

"What is he, some sort of juvenile delinquent?"

"It's not that. It's just, he's . . ." She held out her hands. How could she say it? "You know, Mom, *you* know, he's the kind of boy who . . . he doesn't *ask*," she said fiercely. "He just . . . he does what he wants, and he expects you to want it, too."

"That's one boy you ought to stay away from," her father said.

"I am!"

"And what about your friend Seth?" he said.

"What about him?" Her hands got slippery. She wiped them again. "I don't want to talk about Seth."

"I thought that's what we were talking about."

"Yes, but not that way! I'm not going to talk about Seth."

"Oh, you're not?"

"No, I'm not! I don't want to say personal things about him."

"You want an awful lot, don't you?"

"No," Finn said. "Not so much. Just to be treated like a real person."

They looked at each other. Finn forced herself not to drop her eyes. "You used to listen to me," her father said.

"I know I did, Dad. I still do."

"No—" He shook his head. "You do what you want."

"Please, Dad . . . I'm growing up . . . I don't do it to make you feel bad. You and Mom raised me right. Don't you believe that? You don't have to worry about me."

"I wish I could think so," he said. He had dropped the newspaper, and it had come unrolled. He was folding it, pressing down the pages, as if it mattered. To give him something to do with his hands, Finn thought.

Seeing him that way, his mouth turned up in an ironic, defensive smile, for the first time she felt his vulnerability. Felt that he was hanging on to his position—I am the father!—but that he was no more secure than she was. How strange! It hurt her to see him like that. She had always thought of him as so . . . *powerful,* all-powerful, and now in that moment she saw in the way his hands fumbled at the paper, in that little smile, that he was doubtful of his power.

"Dad," she said. He looked up. "Can't we talk? You know, not just yell at each other. . . . Look, if Seth wasn't nineteen, would you let me see him?"

"It would depend on a lot of things."

"What things?"

"What sort of person he was. I don't want you hanging around with bums. . . . "

She laughed. "Seth's not a bum! He's a hardworking person. You, of all people, should respect that, Dad! What if he was eighteen? Would you let me see him then?"

"There're other things—"

"Oh, I know. He's Jim's brother. But you know yourself that's so unfair. Come on, Dad, you wouldn't want to be judged in your character because of what someone else did."

"No, I wouldn't," he said.

"There!" she said. "But that's what you're doing."

"Don't put words in my mouth."

"I'm not! I'm just pointing out to you—"

"Please . . . please . . ." Her mother sat up. "Can't we stop this bickering? I'm so tired of it! Sometimes I think things haven't been really right since Maggie moved. We've all been upset . . ." She held up a photo. "Look," she said wistfully, "here we all were last summer, all together . . . just last summer."

Her mother's sadness reached Finn. Impulsively she bent over, taking her mother's hand. They hadn't touched in a long time. "Mom . . . it's okay," she said. She didn't know what she meant exactly, only that her mother didn't have to be sad. Didn't have to be scared for her. They couldn't go back to last summer . . . none of them could . . . but still, it was okay.

"Mom . . ." Her mother looked up at her, almost as if she were waiting for Finn to set things right. "Mom

. . . I love you, you know." She kissed her mother's cheek.

"Finn." Her mother put her hand up to Finn's face and kissed her back. "There, we're even." There was a softness in her voice that had been missing for a long time. "Oh, why can't we all make up?" she said. "Just stop being mad at each other."

"I want to," Finn said. "I want to stop. Dad—" She knelt on the bed, reaching out both hands. "You and me—let's make up, too. Don't be mad at me anymore. I'm your daughter."

"That's why I care what you do," he said. "If I didn't love you, it wouldn't make any difference to me."

"I love you, too," she said. Her eyes were wet. She got her arms around him and hugged him. "Remember me? I'm Finn." He was stiff in her arms. "Come on, Dad, hug me," she cried. And right then she felt something happening, something changing. She felt it like a wind rushing past her, brushing her skin.

Her father put his arms around her, still stiff at first, then after a moment he hugged her, held her, hugged her again.

Finn reached for a tissue from the bedside table. "Sniffle, sniffle," she said, laughing and wiping her eyes.

"Better give me one of those, too," her father said. They were all sniffling and smiling and wiping their eyes. And then her father said, "If you go out now, when will you come back?"

"Three o'clock?" she said quickly. Her heart started that incredible pounding.

Her father nodded. "Three o'clock. Not a minute later. No excuses. Home by three."

"I'll be here," she said. "You can depend on it."

As soon as she was outside, she started running. It was nearly noon. They'd hardly have any time. But it was okay. It was wonderful. She got the bus downtown just in time. Then she ran the rest of the way to Seth's room.

21

"Here, these are for you." Finn handed Seth a bunch of pussy willows. "An old guy was selling them on the corner."

"Thanks," he said, putting them in the jar with the bittersweet. He swung her around. "I feel great today! I've been waiting for you. I dreamt about you!"

"Really?" she said, laughing.

"Yes. A sexy dream. Take off your jacket, your hands are so hot."

"I'm steaming! I ran from downtown." She threw off her jacket and scarf. "You have to get a bike, Seth. The weather's getting so good, pretty soon we can ride out to Green Lakes for picnics. It's beautiful out there."

"Car first. A bike'll never get me to Maine."

"Maine," she said. "I keep forgetting about Maine. Are you really going to go?"

"Yes," he said. "One of these days."

"I don't want you to."

"It's not for a long time. Let's not talk about it now." He pulled her down on his lap on the bed. They started hugging and kissing, then fell down together. She put her arms around his neck.

"I love this room," she said. She thought everything was beautiful. The peaked ceiling, the dusty diamond-shaped window, the green walls, even the bare wooden floor.

They kissed and kissed. It was bliss! "I'm going to take off your clothes," he said.

"No," she said.

"Come on," he said. "I want you to. Your jeans and shirt, at least. It's nicer. It's just like being in your bathing suit."

"Well," she said.

"Sure it is," he said. He started to unbutton her blouse.

"I'll do it myself," she said.

"Spoilsport." But he was grinning. He threw off all his clothes.

Again they kissed and kissed, and touched each other. She was happy. She loved being so close . . . the feeling of their bodies touching . . . the warmth of his skin. . . . It was like sunshine . . . like being in the middle of a meadow . . . green grass . . . flowers . . . birds singing. . . .

He rolled half on top of her, working his legs between hers.

She looked up at him, surprised, then uneasy.

"Hello," she said, the green grass fading. "What's going on?"

"What do you think? Something nice is going to happen." He kept working her legs apart with his leg.

"Seth, wait. . . ." She spoke softly. "Listen . . . don't *do* that."

"Wait for what?"

"You know I don't want to . . . come on, honey. . . ." She was still speaking softly, not wanting to hurt his feelings.

"Don't be scared," he said. "I know what I'm doing."

"No, I'm not scared," she said, but she recognized that she *was* scared. But not of sex. Of *him*. It was that smile on his face. He was smiling and smiling. She almost didn't recognize him. That devilish, delighted smile. She didn't like that smile. She didn't like the way he was pressuring her. She didn't like not feeling *safe* with him.

"Lots of people are scared the first time," he said.

"That's *funny*," she said. "Don't you think it's funny? You think I'm afraid to do what my parents are afraid I'm *not* afraid to do." Instinctively she wanted to talk, to make him talk, to divert him.

"Finn, will you *relax!*"

"No," she said. "Listen, we agreed—I told you I didn't want to—"

"We didn't agree on anything," he said quickly. The smile had faded. "Come on, man, give yourself a chance."

"A chance at what?" She had both hands against his chest, holding him away from her. He was heavy. She was beginning to feel smothered, almost desperate. *This is Seth,* she told herself.

"A chance to see what life's all about." He pulled at her underwear.

"Stop it, Seth!"

"It'll be wonderful, Finn, I promise you."

"*Seth.* No!"

"You're serious, aren't you?" he said, pausing and looking down at her.

"I'm dead serious. Will you get off me? Please!" Her throat felt tight. "You know how I feel. I told you!"

"That's just talk, man."

"Stop calling me man!" Weirdly that made her angry, and anger made her strong. She gave him a shove. "Get off me. I mean it!"

"Jesus, are you a mule!" They were really fighting now. "You don't even know what you're missing! Do you think there's something nasty about making love? The whole world's been doing it for ten million years. It ought to be a proven thing, by now."

"Prove it with someone else," she choked. "The way I heard it, both people are supposed to want to."

"And the way I heard it," he snapped back, "girls aren't playing prude anymore." He had on that face she didn't know—a grinning, intense, domineering face. "Will you just let me—"

"No," she said. "No! No!"

He sat up, glaring at her. "I must be off the wall. My father always said I did things the hard way. Seth Hardhead. Seth's way is the dumb way. Falling for a fifteen-year-old girl. Now that's just plain dumb, Finn. Dumb," he said. "Dumb. Dumb, dumb, dumb, *dumb!*"

"I thought you were someone special," she said, holding back tears. God! She didn't want to cry.

"And I thought you were," he said. "But I guess you think it should all be Finn, Finn, Finn. Do you have any idea how I feel? You think it's right to shoot off into the wall?"

"You're twisting everything around!" She scrambled off the bed, then pulled on her clothes as fast as she could. "I'm getting out of here!"

He leaped up and pulled on his jeans. "You stay right here! We're going to talk about this."

"You go to hell," she said. "You hear me? Go to hell!" She ran out and down the stairs, those nasty narrow broken-down stairs, cold as death and smelling of cat pee.

"Finn!" he called. "Come back here."

He must have opened the door to shout after her. She imagined him on the landing in his bare feet. She had noticed today that his feet were long and thin. "Ugly feet," she whispered to herself. "Ugly, ugly feet."

22

So that's it . . . so that's it . . . Those were the words racing through Finn's mind as she walked down Tar Street, away from Seth's room. *So that's it.* She was stunned. It was all over between them. All over. Just like the stories—where if the boy couldn't get what he wanted, he turned nasty and blamed the girl. *So that's it.* Those three words seemed to sum up everything.

When she got home, her parents had just come in from a drive. It was three o'clock. She was right on time. She thought back to the morning. It seemed so long ago that she'd kissed her mother and father.

Her parents were going to eat out and take in a movie. She was invited. "No, I can't. I have homework." Around five o'clock they went out. Finn didn't do any work. She got into bed and turned off the light. She lay in the dark room thinking about herself and Seth.

Had she been wrong to say no? What if she'd just let it happen? It would have made Seth happy. And her? He thought it would make her happy, too. So did Vida. She remembered a long time ago saying to Vida, *Too young, too soon, too important.* And with just as much conviction, Vida had said, *You're wrong, Finn.* She'd never thought she was, but now . . . God, how could she tell? Her legs trembled with exhaustion. What if she *was* wrong? Why not? What made *her* infallible? What made her know so positively?

SEX—the big little word. The little giant of a word. It had come between them. Was that right? Sex had brought them closer, too. She remembered the first time she was in his room, lying on the bed, his back trembling beneath her hand. . . .

She thought about their moments together . . . all the good times . . . and then this one, bad terrible time. . . . What he had said . . . what she had said. . . . He had accused her . . . as if she were guilty of some crime. . . . The crime of *not* . . . the crime of *no* . . .

She felt she hated him. "I hate him," she said out loud. But as soon as she said it, she thought just the opposite. She was still in love. She still loved him. She wanted to smile, then she felt like crying. Her emotions were impossible.

It all went round in her head . . . round and round and round and round . . . in dizzying circles. Even sleep didn't end it. All night she dreamed about it. Still, it was better sleeping than lying awake. She slept a lot the next few days. She seemed to sleepwalk through school.

The whole week was weathery. The wind blew almost

constantly, thunder rumbled in the distance, and at night the rain came. The streets were foggy, and the rain poured down in slanting silver sheets. Finn felt fragile—as if the smallest glance could shake her . . . suspended—as if she were waiting for something to happen.

One night she stood by the window watching the dim, empty street below. A dog barked. A lonely sound, coming to her through the dark, wet night.

Friday morning it was still raining. "This rain must be making you gloomy," her mother said at breakfast.

Finn tried to smile. "I guess so."

Later, walking home from school with Vida, sharing Vida's plastic umbrella, she said, "At least I made up with my parents." It was cold comfort. She bent her head under the umbrella. The world looked murky, gray. The rain . . . or maybe just her mood. There was a murky feeling in her heart. Everything was gray and dim. No clean hard edges, not even to her feelings. If only she could be simply furious, or disgusted, with Seth. If only she could cleanly hate him for being a rotten creep. But she couldn't, because he wasn't a rotten creep. He was Seth, and she loved him, and she felt sick about the way things had turned out.

She was talking under her breath. Vida had heard it all half a dozen times already. "I don't know, Finn," she said, "what'd you expect of the poor guy?"

"Poor guy!"

"Well, I mean, you know how guys are."

Finn yanked the umbrella handle toward her. "Is there just one way boys are? Is Seth just like Jerry? Just like Paul?"

"Well, sure," Vida said, "in a way that's true. You know it, Finn."

"I don't know it," Finn said loudly, stubbornly. "How come they're all alike, and we aren't?"

"I really don't know," Vida said, "but that's the way it is."

"I don't believe it!" Abruptly she ducked out from under the umbrella. If Vida was right then she, Finn, was just a damn fool. A total idiot to think she could have had more with Seth—or any boy, ever—than she had right now. And what she had right now was nothing.

"Want to stop for something?" Vida said as they approached Nick's Pizzeria.

"No," Finn said.

"I'm hungry," Vida said. "Ever since Paul and I broke up, I've been eating like a horse. I'm hungry all the time. I gained five pounds." But she didn't sound displeased. She patted her breasts. "I think I put it all on right here."

"I don't want to go in there," Finn said. "Not there, Vida! If you want something to eat, come up to my house. My mother made a roast last night. Rare. You can have it with mustard and lettuce." She didn't know why she was going on like that. She wasn't the least bit hungry. The thought of food, in fact, sickened her. This morning she'd barely gotten down a glass of orange juice, and at lunchtime all she'd had was an ice cream sandwich.

"Well, get back under the umbrella, will you?" Vida said. "You're getting soaked."

"It doesn't matter," Finn said.

"You're so depressed," Vida said. "*You* can always make up. Not like Paul and me. We're through. I cried the first two nights. But now—" She shrugged. "It's funny, Finn, it's a really lonesome feeling to wake up in the morning and think I have no one to see in school. But I don't miss *Paul*. It's just I'm so used to knowing I'll see him or talk to him on the phone, go places with him. . . ."

Finn sloshed through a puddle. The cars passing them had on their headlights. "Don't you just hate this weather?" Finn said with sudden ferocity. "I hate this!"

"I sort of like rain," Vida said. "It's cozy."

Finn fell silent, remembering the first time she'd gone to Seth's room and the sound of the rain on the roof. That was exactly what she'd thought. Cozy. She could feel her eyes filling. "I never thought he'd be like that," she said after a while.

"You keep saying that," Vida said.

"Do I?"

"Yes, you said that before. I could have told you, Finn."

"No, you couldn't! You don't know Seth." She sneezed several times. "That's all I need," she said, feeling more depressed by the moment. "If I get sick, I might as well cut my throat. I'll really go crazy if I have to stay home with nothing to do." Her throat tightened. "Oh, I'm just feeling sorry for myself," she exclaimed. "Don't listen to me." They turned onto their block. "Are you still hungry, Vida?"

"I'll go home and get something," Vida said.

"Okay," Finn said. But she didn't want Vida to leave. She didn't want to go into her empty house and wander around, thinking of Seth. "Sure you don't want to come up?"

"Well . . ." Vida half laughed. "I sort of expect a call from Jerry."

"Jerry Demas?"

"Mmm," Vida said, not meeting Finn's eyes.

"That's nice," Finn said.

"You don't mind?"

"Vida, why should I mind? Jerry and I haven't even talked for weeks. He's the last person I'm thinking of."

"Oh, good, I'm glad. I felt sort of guilty. I mean, I know how you feel about Seth, but I kept thinking, Well, she and Jerry had something going—"

"No, we never did. Not really."

Vida went up on the Barnowskis' porch and shook out her umbrella. "See you tomorrow." Finn waved and went inside. As she went up the stairs, she heard the phone ringing. She didn't run. What for? It was still ringing when she went inside, but it stopped just as she picked up the receiver. She stood there listening to the buzzing, overwhelmed by the feeling that it had been Seth. Oh, God, she wanted to see him.

She took an apple from the bowl of fruit on the table. If she wanted to see him, why didn't she just go down to the factory and wait for him to come out after work? Such a simple thought. Such a simple idea. I'll do it, she thought. She stared at the apple, then put it down.

Long before she got to the factory, she smelled it. All around it were blocks of nothing but rubble where slum housing had been torn down. A fat man jangling a bunch of keys came out and climbed into a Flips Chips truck. He looked over at Finn. She walked up and down, hunched inside her raincoat. What would she say to Seth? She didn't know. Not the faintest idea. She'd say something. He'd say something. They'd talk. That was all that mattered.

She stared at the littered ground. Her sneakers were getting soaked. A whistle blew, and a clot of people pushed out the door. Men, women . . . lunchboxes banging against their legs. They headed for cars parked on the street, or for the corner bus stop.

Seth came out. He was walking slowly, his head down, his knapsack over one shoulder. A wave of emotion went through Finn. "Seth," she said. He looked up. A painful smile crossed his face.

"Hello," he said. "What are you doing here?"

"Oh, nothing." Finn shrugged. "I just came down."

They started walking. He smelled of grease and chips, and walked slowly, without the bounce she was used to. Was that what working did to a person?

"You look like you worked hard today," she said. She struggled not to feel sympathetic. He'd wronged her. He'd been so wrong! Just tried to do what he wanted with her, and the hell with the way she felt or what she wanted.

"It's a dog of a job," he said. "I hate it. I'm going to quit."

"Oh." She felt foolish, young, innocent. She felt at a disadvantage. Not his equal. He knew about the world. He worked. He quit jobs, took other jobs. He had a weary look to his face. It silenced her.

"What's up?" he said.

She shook her head. "Nothing. I wanted to see you."

"I called you. You weren't home."

"Today?" she said.

"No, yesterday on my break. I thought you might be home early."

"No, I did some shopping for my mother."

They walked in silence for a while. At last he said, "I guess you want to talk about Sunday?"

"Yes." She wanted to be very angry at him. She *was* angry. But she felt sad and confused, too.

"I'm sorry," he said. "I acted like a total ass. I came on like gangbusters."

She'd had so much prepared to tell him. How unfair he'd been, how disappointed she'd been in him. . . . She didn't say any of it. She just felt sorry for him. She put her hand on his arm.

"Seth—"

He looked at her and smiled faintly. "I really was bad to you."

"Oh—" She hated seeing him this way, so quiet, so subdued.

"Here's where I get my bus," he said. They stood in the Plexiglas shelter together. "Maybe we can do something tomorrow," he said.

"Yes, maybe," she said.

"What did you do this week?" he asked.

"Changed my room all around, slept a lot. Mostly hung out feeling awful and hating you."

"Are you still mad at me?" The same thing he'd said that time in the War Memorial.

"I don't know," she said. "I was, awfully—"

"Oh, were you ever." Then for the first time he really

smiled. "Left me flat-footed. Did you hear me calling you?"

"You didn't expect me to come back?"

"I don't know what I expected. I don't think I was at my best."

"What'd *you* do this week," she said.

"Worked and wrote letters. I was feeling really blue. Mad at you. I told myself, Seth, forget it. Get out of this town. I wrote to a couple I know, Jane and Neely. They're farming in Vermont. I asked them if they wanted a willing hand."

"Really?" she said politely. Her heart had immediately started to pound with alarm when he said Vermont. Did he mean it? Was he going to Vermont? "Did you hear from them? Oh, I guess it's too soon to get an answer."

She stuck her hand out into the rain and then put it against her burning face. She wanted him to say that it didn't matter if his friends answered him or not. That he had no intention of going away. She stared out into the street, watching the cars throwing up water as they passed.

"Neely . . . what a funny name," she said suddenly. She wanted him to talk about Neely and Jane. Who were they?

"Yes, that's his last name," Seth said. "I've known him for years, big guy, nobody ever calls him anything but Neely. His first name is Dexter."

"Ahhh," she said, nodding, as if that explained everything. She heard herself. . . . She sounded amused . . .

very cool. How could she sound that way and feel so despairing?

His bus was coming. "I'll call you about tomorrow," he said. "Okay?"

"Okay." Her eyes filled. She felt that he would never call her. He would forget, and then Neely would write back and say yes, come to the farm. And Seth would pack his knapsack and go. He wouldn't even remember to say good-bye to her.

"Finn?" He bent toward her. The bus passed them. "You're upset," he said. He put his arm around her. "Don't get upset." And when she didn't say anything, "Want me to tell you a joke?"

"A joke?" She stared at him. Her cheeks blazed. "Don't treat me like a child!" Furiously she shook off his arm. "Why do you always make me feel so stupid?"

"I don't know what you mean." He moved a step away from her.

"Yes, you do. In your room, that whole thing—why did you do that?"

"I don't know," he said.

"Yes! You know," she insisted. "I told you—didn't I tell you how I felt?"

"But I thought—"

"You didn't believe me," she said. Her anger had come roaring back. She gave herself to it. She ignored the half-pained smile on his face. No! Let her have her say! She needed to say it. She didn't want to think about him now. If she was hurting him, that was too bad! He had hurt her too much to just let it go.

"No, you didn't believe me," she repeated. "You humored me. You pretended to believe me. 'Sure, Finn, sure, if that's the way you feel, that's okay with me. We won't do anything you don't want to do.' Then you went ahead anyway and tried to do everything you wanted!"

"Well, I thought you were just saying that." He dug his hands into his pockets.

"No, I don't understand you. Why would I just say it?"

"Girls do—"

"No," she said. "No. Why do you say such a terrible thing? I never faked you out. Whatever I felt, I told you. We talked about it. You remember! Why didn't you believe me? What does that make me? I thought you had feeling for me, I thought you loved me—"

"I do—"

"No! If you loved me, you wouldn't think I was a liar."

"I don't!" he said. "I don't think you're a liar. Jesus! Where'd you get that idea?"

She stared at him. It seemed so obvious to her. "From you," she said.

"No," he said. "It's just that—everyone knows you have to convince some girls—" His face was reddening. "Okay, I know I didn't act too wonderfully. But under the circumstances . . . that's a very tense situation for a man."

"But you made it tense," she said, remembering that other time, that beautiful time.

"No, I don't want to accept that. You came to my room—"

"You invited me, Seth."

"—and got in bed with me—"

"That's so unfair," she said. "You kept wheedling me and coaxing me—"

"—and we did so much—"

Her eyes filled again. "Remember the first time, Seth? The first time I came to your room, and we—" She stopped, wrapping her arms around herself. Another bus passed. It was dusk. "You said something about that first time. You said—" She bit her lip. She didn't want to repeat it.

"What?" he said. "What'd I say?"

"Don't you remember?"

"No, I said so many things."

"You said, Did I think it was right for you to shoot off into the wall."

"Oh, that."

"Yes, that." She faced him. "It was so ugly what you said. It meant that day, that first time was—nothing."

"It was beautiful," he said. "I just said that. I wanted to hurt you."

"*Why?*" She leaned against the smeared wall of the shelter.

"We were fighting—Jesus, what about you? You were mad, weren't you?"

"Yes!"

"Well, so was I. And when I get mad, I want to strike out. So I did."

"But . . . you didn't mean it?"

"No, Finn, no, I didn't mean it."

"I'm glad."

"Are we friends again?" he said.

"I want to be," she said. "Do you?"

"Yes. Very much."

The rain was still coming down. "Then . . . let's shake on it," she said, putting out her hand.

"I'd rather kiss," he said, but he took her hand. They shook hands ceremoniously. Then they leaned toward each other and kissed.

23

"Finn?" Maggie said on the phone. "I'm having a party to celebrate a year Jim and I have known each other. You're invited. Next Friday night. Okay?" Maggie sounded the way she alway did.

"I'll come," Finn said. "Thanks. Is Seth invited?" she added.

"Definitely," Maggie said. "See you then."

It was a week and a half since Finn had met Seth at the factory gate, but they hadn't seen each other since. He had called to say he was working overtime, and he'd let her know as soon as things eased up. She wondered if he'd come to Maggie's party. She hoped so.

The night of the party Finn went to Maggie's early to help get things set up. "You look great," Maggie said. Finn was wearing new blue-and-white pin-striped pants with a pin-striped vest over a long-sleeved blouse.

"You do, too," Finn said. "Dragon Lady." Maggie

was all in green—a long green gown, jade earrings, green eye shadow, and even green shoes.

"Did you know I asked Mom and Dad to come to the party?" Maggie handed Finn two bowls of food to put on the table.

"I know," Finn said. "You're crazy. What ever made you do that?"

"Crazy like Einstein," Maggie said, setting out paper plates. "Mom would've come."

Finn nodded. "That's true. Dad is the holdout."

" 'Not till they're married,' " Maggie said, making her voice gruff.

Finn laughed. "Anyway, he got on the phone and said hello to you, didn't he?"

Maggie looked pleased. "Sure did."

There were voices in the hall, and people started arriving. Finn kept watching for Seth.

Jim moved around with a tray of Coors. His curls were damp, his round face glistened, even his glasses shone as if they'd just been washed.

People helped themselves to food. More people arrived. There was music on the stereo. "Where's the champagne, Maggie?" one of her friends asked. "You gotta have champagne to celebrate."

"We open it at eleven twenty-two," Maggie said. "That's the exact minute Jim and I met."

Finn didn't know most of the people, but she recognized Toby, the Future Kindergarten Teacher, with her gold chains. She was looking around, too—for Seth?

"Hi," Finn said. "Did you ever get your MG?"

Toby looked at her. "Have we met?"

"I'm Maggie's sister. Finn. We met a few months ago."

"Maggie's sister?" Toby looked blank for a moment. "Oh, now I remember. Maggie's little sister—you look different." She bit one of her golden chains. "I thought you were younger."

"I was," Finn said, laughing. She drifted over to the window and looked down at the street. Raining again, but very lightly. The street glistened blackly. A man came around the corner. Seth? She pressed her face against the glass. No.

"Hi, there." A tall young man smiled at Finn. He was holding a can of beer. "I heard you laughing. You've got a smashing laugh. I'm Kevin," he added.

"I'm Finn."

"Hi, Finn."

"Hi, Kevin."

"Neat party, isn't it? I think Jim and Maggie are a neat couple. What do you say?"

"I like them all right," Finn said, smiling.

"Just all right? Aren't you a friend?"

"Oh, sure, I've known Maggie for a long time."

"Well, I just met her and I think she's smashing."

From the corner of her eye she saw Seth. He'd arrived without her noticing. He was wearing a blue denim shirt with a sun embroidered on the back. He and Jim were shaking hands. She raised her hand, and he saw her.

"Kevin, my friend just came," she said.

He followed her eyes. "Wouldn't you know," he said. "That's my luck."

She and Seth moved toward each other. "Oh, I'm glad you could make it," she said. "Did you just come from work? Or the barbershop? You look like you had a haircut."

"I did," he said. "Yesterday. I like your vest."

"Matches my pants." She preened a little.

He lifted her hair off her shoulder. "Nice this way." She was wearing it loose.

"Well," she said. "Here we are."

"Here we are."

"How are you?" she said.

"Oh . . . I've been sort of depressed. Because of us. Did we really make up?"

"I thought so," she said.

They moved into a corner near the window. He leaned against the wall, his hands in his back pockets. "No, you know what I mean. The way we were before."

Toby came toward them, her arms out. "Seth!" She hugged him. "Maggie said you'd be here. I haven't seen you in ages. How are you, baby? God! You're looking great!"

Seth laughed. "You're looking good yourself. How's the teaching business?"

Finn started to move away. Seth caught her hand. "Don't go. I want to talk to you."

"I'll be here." She went to the stereo and stood there, listening to the music. People were sitting on the floor, perching on chairs, eating, talking and sipping cans of beer. Empty cans and paper plates were filling up the yellow plastic pail Jim had set inside the kitchen door.

"Having fun?" Maggie said, breezing past Finn.

"Sure," Finn said.

Seth came over and touched her arm. "Let's cut out for a little while. Go for a walk." They left the apartment. Downstairs they stood on the steps under the overhang. The rain was very soft and warm.

"I've been thinking," he said, "when I go to Vermont to work with Jane and Neely—"

Her stomach jolted. "Did you hear from them?"

"Yes, they want me to come in July."

May, she thought. Then June. Then July. She didn't know what it would feel like when he went. It would hurt. Hurt a lot. "If you go—"

"*When*—"

"—will we write each other?"

"Do you like to write letters?" he said.

"I don't mind."

"I'm terrible about it," he said. "But I could try."

"I hope you do."

He stroked her neck. "Let's go to my room. Walk over—"

She shook her head. "We'll just end up fighting. I don't want to fight with you."

"We won't fight," he said.

"Oh, we will," she said. "You know we will, Seth. Because it'll just be the same, won't it?"

"No, it's going to be different." He took out a cigarette and lit it. She remembered the first time she'd seen him take out a cigarette. At the War Memorial. And their first kiss. The first time he drove her home. The first time they were in his room. A lot of firsts.

"Remember the War Memorial?" she said. "The non-concert? I was just thinking of all the things we've done . . . all the first times."

"You're nostalgic," he said.

"I know," she said, "but it's nice to look back and think—we did that, we did this, that was the first time . . ."

"Our first fight," he said.

"And our second," she added.

They started walking down the street. "Finn, really, I've been doing a lot of thinking. I'll tell you—I always thought we'd make love—" He glanced at her. They were walking side by side, just brushing against each other. "For a long time now any girl I go with, I sleep with."

"Did they all want to?" she said. She couldn't be the only girl in the world who wanted to wait until she was older.

"I always thought so," he said. "I don't know, maybe they were just going along. I always figured the thing to do was try, just keep trying. You know. If at first you don't succeed . . . that's the male creed."

"That's a poem," she said. "I don't understand. What does it mean?"

"It means that the macho thing to do with a girl is never take no for an answer. Just keep trying. Wear her down one way or the other."

"That's ugly," she said.

"I know," he said. "I've never really thought about it before. A lot of things. Like, I was thinking about the first time. It *was* beautiful. So why did I start pressing you? The only thing I can figure is that somehow I've gotten the idea that sleeping with a girl is the *only* thing that counts."

They walked in silence for a while. "I've missed you,"

he said. He flicked away his cigarette. "It hurts me. I feel bad about things. I want us to go on."

She leaned toward him. "Won't it happen again, though?"

"No," he said, "it doesn't have to be that way."

"But how will we be with each other? I mean, about sex?"

"We'll be happy together," he said. "We'll do everything we want to do, and nothing that both of us don't want to do."

"Really?"

"Yes," he said. "That's what I've been thinking about. I'll tell you something. I haven't slept with a girl in over a year. I've survived. Better than that! It's been good with you. We don't have to—there are other things to do that'll make us both feel good."

"Like the first time?"

"Yes, that's what I mean."

He put his arm around her. "Should we try?" he said. She heard the way he put it. *Try*, as if it were an experiment, something with an uncertain outcome. He wasn't as sure as he sounded. She used to think everything was simple. Black and white. Right and wrong. Falling in love was supposed to be simple.

"Let's try," she said. "Yes, let's."

They embraced, holding each other tightly. Finn put her face against his neck and tightened her arms around him.

After a while they kept walking. The rain fell. Had anyone asked Finn just then how she felt she would have had to say, Happy and sad. Sad and happy.

24

"Finn. . . ."

Finn heard Seth calling, but she didn't see him. Vida nudged her. "Over there, Finn, in that gray car." He was leaning out the window of a car parked in front of the school.

Finn ran down the last few steps. "Hello! Whose car?"

"Mine. Like it?" It was small and old with rusted fenders.

Vida patted Seth's hand. "Nice, Seth."

"You bought it," Finn said. "I can't believe it. You really bought a car at last. He's been talking about it for weeks," she said to Vida.

"This girl wanted me to get a bike," Seth said.

"Then we could go riding together."

"A car is better," Vida said.

"Tell her, Vida."

Finn leaned down and rubbed her nose hard against Seth's. "You two are ganging up on me."

"Do you have time to go for a ride?" Seth said.

"Well, Vida and I were going to do some shopping—"

"No, no," Vida said, "that's okay. We can shop tomorrow or Saturday. No problem. Go ahead."

"You sure?" Finn said. "Seth could drive us downtown, show off his new car."

"Vida's sure," Seth said. "Aren't you, Vida?"

"Absolutely," Vida said. "Talk to you later, Finn. Bye-bye, Seth." She walked away.

Finn slid in next to Seth. He drove down the street. "This beats walking, doesn't it?"

Finn dumped her books in the backseat. "How old is this car?" She inspected the dashboard. "I hope your transmission doesn't go. Mom just had hers done, and it cost a bundle."

"Eleven years old," he said. "But it's a Volvo, built like a tank. It'll last forever, especially if I get it out of this salt country."

She heard that. Getting out of the salt country meant going somewhere else. "Cars rust out here, all right," she said. "My father says seven years, and they're ready for the graveyard." She pulled her long switch of hair around and chewed on the ends. Damn. She didn't like his talking about going away. Every time he said something about it, she got that same cold drop in her stomach.

"Do you like this?" she said, opening her notebook.

"I did it in Trig." It was a pencil sketch of two figures going up a long flight of stairs on the outside of a big rambly house.

He glanced over. "Nice."

"You and me," she said. "Just in case you didn't guess."

"Let me have it," he said.

"I'll sign it," she said. She took out a pen and with a flourish signed her name. "There. A Finn original."

He didn't laugh. He tucked it in his shirt pocket.

It was a perfect June day. Finn rolled down the windows of the car. "Where are we going?" Seth was driving south out of the city into the Pompey Hills. Everything was soft and green. Water ran in every stream and brook lacing through the hills.

"We'll just drive around for a while," he said.

"Did you pay a lot for the car?"

"Enough," he said. "Maybe I should have shopped around a little more, but I really like these old cars." He patted the steering wheel. "Did you notice my license plate? It's one thirty-six M-A-X. So guess what I've named this baby?"

"Easy," Finn said. "One Thirty-six."

Seth turned off onto a dirt road going up into the hills. They passed farms smelling of manure, and long bare fields. He drove slowly. The road was heaved up from the winter and the spring melt-off. They passed an abandoned farmhouse. The road narrowed. He pulled the car to the side of the road. Around them the uncultivated fields were overgrown with grass and flowers.

They walked up the road hand in hand. There was nothing to be seen but fields on all sides. The silence was intense. Finn could hear it throbbing in her ears. Only the call of birds broke the quiet. She took off her sweater and tied it around her waist.

They left the road and walked into a field, uphill through a mass of dandelions and daisies. "It's so beautiful," she said happily. "I'm really glad we came." She picked a daisy and stuck it in Seth's hair. "Oh, we should walk barefoot, Seth." She took off her shoes and tied them together. "Seth, do it! The grass feels so good." She looked at him. "Why aren't you saying anything?"

"Finn—" He put his hands on her shoulders.

"What is it?" She put another daisy in his hair. "You ought to wear daisies all the time."

"Hey—" He shook her gently. "I've got to tell you something. Are you listening?"

"Sure." She rubbed her nose against his. "Don't be so solemn."

"No, *listen*," he said. "I came to say good-bye."

She looked at him, still smiling, but it was the sort of smile that comes when you hear something terrible. "Good-bye?" she said.

He nodded. "Jane called, and—"

"Jane?"

"Jane and Neely. You know. My friends in—"

"I know. Vermont," she said. "How'd she call you?" she demanded. "You don't have a phone."

"They called Jim, and he got in touch with me. They want me to come to the farm right away.'

"No," she said, twisting away, "you're supposed to go in July." She started walking up the hill again. "It's only June!" she exclaimed.

"Neely hurt himself," Seth said, catching up with her. "He threw out his back. They need me now."

They came to the top of the hill and sat down. The grass was so high that only their heads showed above it. In the distance Finn saw the long silver-gray lake. She didn't speak. It was hot, and Seth took off his shirt.

"You knew I was going to go," he said.

"Yes. Someday," she said. "Not *now*."

"Another month—"

"Another month is a long time," she cried. "I don't want you to go now!" She looked away from him, fighting angry tears.

He turned her head toward him. "I don't want to go, either."

"Then don't!"

"I promised—"

"Oh, what do I care about your promises!" She bent over, covering her head with her hands.

He stroked her back. "Finn, you know I have to do this. Not just for Jane and Neely—"

"I know! I know!" She knew all the reasons. Seth's dream of farming. His need to try himself. Good reasons. When his leaving was something in the future, she could talk about his plans, she could be sympathetic, interested. She could care. She *did* care. Only now it was happening—happening to her.

"Finn, come on . . . please. . . ." He touched the back

of her neck. "It's not easy on me, either . . ." His voice thickened.

She looked up. "Are you crying?"

He shook his head, half smiling. "Not yet. I feel like it."

"Cry!" she said. "I want you to cry! I want you to hurt. I hurt."

"Don't," he said. "I don't want to hurt you."

They embraced and held each other. "Will you miss me?" he said.

"You know I will. Will you miss me?"

"I do already."

"I don't want you to go," she said again. She held him tightly.

"Closer," he said. "Closer!" The ground was warm. Insects buzzed in the grass.

They took off their clothes. Naked, they knelt together, their knees touching. She put her hands on his shoulders. He held her waist. Then they lay down together. There was the smell of crushed grass and dandelions.

Fingers . . . hands . . . lips . . .

"Oh . . . now!" He turned away. He was singing. He always sang. She had her arms around him, her face pressed against his back. She floated in golden circles, spinning higher and higher, the circles narrowing and golden, dazzling.

A hawk soared over them, rising and rising through the hot blue sky.

She kissed his back. "Seth—"

"Yes?"

"Did we just make love? Vida thinks what we do isn't making love."

"Vida doesn't know everything." He lay on his back.

"Do you think the hawk saw us?" Leaning up on her elbow, she pulled a handful of flowers and scattered them over Seth.

"Hawks see everything," he said.

"Watch this, hawk!" She pulled more flowers, handfuls of them, and covered Seth from his thighs to his neck. "My flower boy."

The sun was going down, a chill came into the air. They dressed and walked back to the car.

"I still can't believe you're really going," she said, as they drove down the dirt road.

"I know. I feel the same way." He drove with one hand on the wheel, his other hand linked with hers. "I'll come back. I'll visit."

She nodded.

"You'll have another boyfriend by then."

"I won't."

"You'll see," he said. "You'll love other people."

"Yes," she said, "but not for a long time."

He held her hand tighter.

As they turned the corner onto her street, she said quickly, "Don't say good-bye! I hate good-byes."

He parked the car in front of her house. "Finn—"

She touched her fingers to her lips, then touched his mouth, his hand, the ring she'd given him. They put their arms around each other. They didn't speak, just held each other. When they broke apart, his eyes were wet.

"I won't forget you," he said.

She got out of the car and ran up on the porch. He was still there, looking out the car window, looking at her. She raised her hand. Then, at last, he drove away. She stood there until the car was out of sight. Then she went inside.

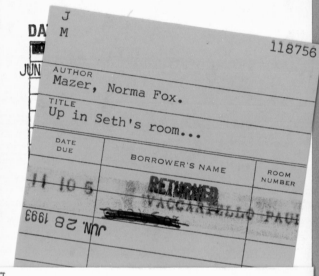